What was he afraid was going to happen if he had sex with her?

Sebastian knew she could deny it all she wanted, but Julie was the happily-ever-after type. So why had she propositioned him out of the blue?

Just then, there was a knock at the hotel-room door. Grateful for the distraction, Sebastian went to answer it. "Yes?"

"Package for Mr. Black."

Sebastian opened the door, tipped the bellman generously and accepted a large box with a fancy ribbon. He removed the lid and peered inside. He laughed at the pair of black cowboy boots, matching black Stetson and brand-new lasso.

At the bottom of the box was a folded note.

"I'm naughtier than you could ever guess, cowboy. Wear this outfit and meet me at Lone Star riding stables on Sunday at 10:00 a.m. That is, if you have the balls.

J.

P.S. Expect the unexpected..."

Blaze™

Dear Reader,

In the first two books of the PERFECT ANATOMY miniseries you met Elle Kingston and Dr. Vanessa Rodriguez, employees of Confidential Rejuvenations, a hush-hush boutique hospital for the crème de la crème in Austin, Texas. You went along for the ride as they found their true loves in Dante Nash and Tanner Doyle. But their best friend, die-hard romantic Julie DeMarco R.N., was left waiting in the wings.

Julie's been nursing a wounded heart, and working at the sexual dysfunction unit at Confidential Rejuvenations hasn't done much to restore her faith in relationships. Then she meets Sebastian Black—one very sexy spin doctor, hired to repair the hospital's scandalous reputation. He's known far and wide for both his charming way with women and for his inability to commit. But the minute Sebastian meets beguiling Julie, he's captivated.

What they don't know is that someone at Confidential Rejuvenations is watching. And waiting. Determined to destroy not only the hospital, but Julie and Sebastian right along with it.

I hope you enjoy *Lethal Exposure*, the conclusion to the PERFECT ANATOMY series. Please look for my next new series, coming out in 2009 from Harlequin Blaze.

Best wishes,

Lori Wilde

LETHAL EXPOSURE

Lori Wilde

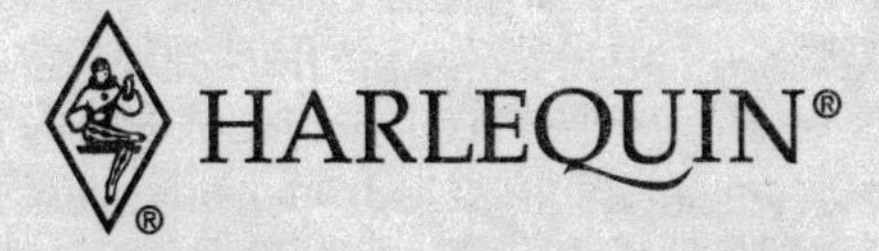

TORONTO • NEW YORK • LONDON
AMSTERDAM • PARIS • SYDNEY • HAMBURG
STOCKHOLM • ATHENS • TOKYO • MILAN • MADRID
PRAGUE • WARSAW • BUDAPEST • AUCKLAND

ISBN-13: 978-0-373-79427-0
ISBN-10: 0-373-79427-4

LETHAL EXPOSURE

This edition published by arrangement with Harlequin Books S.A.

www.eHarlequin.com

Printed in U.S.A.

ABOUT THE AUTHOR

Lori Wilde is the author of forty books. She's been nominated for a RITA® Award and four *Romantic Times BOOKreviews* Reviewers' Choice Awards. Her books have been excerpted in *Cosmopolitan, Redbook* and *Quick & Simple.* Lori teaches writing online through Ed2go. She's an R.N. trained in forensics, and she volunteers at a battered women's shelter.

Books by Lori Wilde

HARLEQUIN BLAZE

30—A TOUCH OF SILK
66—A THRILL TO REMEMBER
106—PACKED WITH PLEASURE
123—AS YOU LIKE IT
152—GOTTA HAVE IT
175—SHOCKINGLY SENSUAL
230—ANGELS AND OUTLAWS*
260—DESTINY'S HAND*
346—MY SECRET LIFE**
399—CROSSING THE LINE***
411—SECRET SEDUCTION***

*The White Star
**The Martini Dares
***Perfect Anatomy

To Brenda Chin, for helming the Blaze line
to great success

1

"SEX SCANDALS, insider media leaks, Mafia connections and homicidal nurses running amok in a hush-hush, celebrity boutique hospital in Austin, Texas? How are you planning on spinning your way out of this one, Sebastian?"

Sebastian Black grinned at his stern secretary, Blanche Santini, like James Bond smirking at Moneypenny. "I'm not a spin doctor," he said. "I'm a highly trained public-relations specialist adept at repairing the tattered reputations of the social elite."

Blanche snorted.

"I'm shocked that you doubt me, Blanche, shocked." He loved teasing her just to see her get bent out of shape. He'd hired Blanche because she reminded him of the doting aunt who'd raised him. He kept her on—even after he discovered she was nothing like his permissive aunt Bunnie—because she was the most efficient secretary he'd ever employed.

"Confidential Rejuvenations' latest disgrace made the front page of the *Inquisitive Tattler.* It's the fourth time this year. Tough case, even for a man with your silver-tongued talents."

"Have you ever known me to fail?"

"First time for everything," Blanche said crisply and dropped the Confidential Rejuvenations file on his desk.

With his smile still firmly entrenched, Sebastian cradled

the back of his head in his palms and propped his feet on his desk. Blanche frowned at his shoes, which were polished to a high sheen. It was all he could do not to settle them back on the floor. The woman worked for him. He wasn't about to let her dictate his behavior.

"Why, Blanche," he drawled. "If I didn't know better I'd think you wanted to see me fall on my ass."

"Charm, poise and sex appeal will only get you so far in life, Mr. Black."

He hated when she called him Mr. Black. It made him feel like his father and he was nothing like his old man. "Don't forget my razor-sharp wit."

Blanche rolled her eyes. "Mark my word, one of these days you're going to get your comeuppance."

"Comeuppance? Which millennium is that from?"

She ignored his comment. "At some point the wine, women and song have got to come to an end."

"It still works for some," Sebastian said.

She waved a hand at the file. "You have a first-class seat booked on the ten a.m. flight to DFW. With the time difference and plane change, you should arrive in Austin on schedule for your dinner appointment with the Confidential Rejuvenations' owners. I checked the weather in Austin, storms are expected this evening so I packed your raincoat. Would you like me to drive you to the airport, sir?"

"No, thanks," Sebastian said. Blanche had driven him to the airport before and she followed the speed limit as if it was one of the Ten Commandments. "I'll get Linc to do it."

"As you wish."

He chuckled, but the minute Blanche was out the door, he dropped his feet to the floor, leaned forward and flipped the file open. Truth was, he loved a challenge of this magnitude.

Sebastian saw himself as a modern-day knight in shining armor. Swooping in on his fire engine–red Ferrari, saving the day with a glib turn of phrase, a wink and a grin for the media and then swooping out again, with money lining his pockets and kudos ringing in his ears. Returning to his lavish 90210 area code and bachelor lifestyle. It was the kind of life he'd daydreamed about as a poor kid growing up on a run-down farm in Bakersfield with his little brother Lincoln, his ditzy, hippie aunt Bunnie and all the other eccentrics at the commune.

He was just about to buzz Lincoln's office when his brother appeared in the doorway, jangling his car keys. Even though Linc was the younger brother, he was a good two inches taller than Sebastian's own six-foot height, and where Sebastian had black hair and black eyes, Lincoln possessed green eyes and auburn hair. They had the same mother. Different fathers. But being half brothers hadn't affected the close bond between them.

Growing up, Sebastian had been the one to look after Linc, get him off to school, make sure he did his homework. He taught him how to ride a bike and then later, drive a car. Aunt Bunnie and her friends had been too busy making clothes out of hemp, drinking wine, spouting liberal politics, writing poetry and playing guitar to pay much attention to what he and Linc were up to.

"Blanche said you needed a lift to LAX." Even though Linc was eleven months back from Iraq, he still kept his hair trimmed in a precision military cut.

"Do you mind? Blanche drives like a prison warden."

"Not at all. It'll give us a chance to talk."

Sebastian pushed back his chair, stood up, took his designer suit jacket off the coatrack and shrugged into it. "What's up?"

"It's about Keeley."

"Did you guys break up?" he asked hopefully.

Sebastian couldn't say he was surprised. While Keeley was a good person, he didn't think she was right for Linc. She was one of those tree-hugging idealists who chided Sebastian for leaving "a big carbon footprint." Whatever the hell that meant. He shrugged. Bottom line, she thought he should drive a Prius and live in a hut made out of manure and eat berries and twigs. Since Keeley was a peacenik and Linc was a soldier, he'd just been waiting for the sonic boom.

He tucked the Confidential Rejuvenations file into his wheeled carry-on bag and spied the present he had tucked away for Linc. He'd been waiting for the right moment to make him an equal partner in the PR company and give him the solid gold nameplate he'd had made for Linc's desk. He snapped the case shut.

Sebastian crossed to the door, pulling the suitcase behind him and clamped his brother on the shoulder. "Don't worry about Keeley. Plenty of fish in the Pacific Ocean. I'll take you out when I get back from Austin. We'll hit all the trendy clubs and get rip-roaring drunk."

Linc met Sebastian's eyes. "Keeley and I didn't break up."

Uh-oh. His brother had that defiant expression on his face that he used when they were kids and Sebastian told him to do something and Linc wasn't of a mind to obey. His brother was generally a pretty accommodating guy, but when he dug in his heels, he dug in his heels. Sebastian couldn't count the number of wrestling matches they'd had as he'd imposed his will on his younger sibling. Linc had never won, but he'd come damn close a time or two.

"No?" Sebastian turned and started toward the elevator, and his shoes suddenly felt heavy, as if he was trudging through mud.

Linc hurried after him. "I know you two don't get along."

"Of course we get along." Sebastian stepped into the elevator and Linc followed. "I get along with everyone."

"On the surface, yeah, because you're great at keeping up appearances, but I know Keeley rubs you the wrong way."

Sebastian punched the button for the parking lot. "Hey, I don't have to sleep with her. If you like her..."

Linc hardened his jaw. "I want you to make more of an effort to see her side of things."

"Look, she's entitled to her opinion, I'm entitled to mine. We don't have to like each other."

"Could you do it for me?"

"Why push us on each other, Linc? This affair will burn out and then you'll have a new girlfriend. I can't be best buddies with all of them."

"You're wrong about that."

Sebastian felt a cold prickle of apprehension slide down his spine. "What do you mean?"

"I wanted you to be the first to know."

He didn't want to ask because he feared the answer, but Linc had a hand on his shoulder. "Know what?"

"Keeley and I are getting married. We've set a date for April. I want you to be my best man."

That grabbed Sebastian by the short hairs. He jerked his gaze to Linc. "You're what?"

His brother wasn't backing down. "You heard me."

"Aw, come on, buddy. You can't be serious."

"I am."

"You're not thinking clearly. Marriage is a huge step and April is only six months away. Why so fast? You've got your whole life ahead of you."

"We're getting married in Austin where her parents live. They want to throw us an engagement party at the end of the month. I can give you their address if you'd like to drop by and meet them while you're in town. Keeley's father is the one who recommended us to Confidential Rejuvenations."

"I appreciate the recommendation her father threw our way, but you don't have to marry Keeley over it," Sebastian joked.

Linc shot him a chiding glance. "Keeley says she'll make an effort to get along with you, if you'll make an effort to get along with her."

"But come on, marriage?"

"She wants you to like her."

It was as if they were having parallel conversations, both talking but neither really hearing the other. "You can't be getting married. You're barely twenty-five and she's what? Twenty? Twenty-one? She's not even through college. That's way too young to get married."

Especially to someone as uptight and uncompromising as Keeley Marshall.

Linc stopped beside his silver Toyota Camry. "My mind is made up, can't you just be happy for us?"

Guilt chewed at him. He wanted to be happy for his brother, he really did, but whenever Sebastian thought about marriage he got a tight choking feeling in his throat. Reaching up, he loosened his tie. "Dude, you've got a good ten years of bachelorhood left in you. Ten years you can never get back. You can always get married."

"I love her, man."

Sebastian raised his palms. "You just think you're in love. You come back from Iraq after seeing a lot of scary things. You're vulnerable, horny and first thing out of the box you meet Keeley. It's chemistry and circumstances. That's all."

"I know what I feel," Linc insisted stubbornly and unlocked his car door with a push of the keypad.

Sebastian tossed his carry-on bag into the backseat and climbed in the passenger side, shaking his head as his brother slipped behind the wheel. He snapped his seat belt into place. "How many women have you slept with?"

"What's that got to do with anything?"

"A hell of a lot."

"It's none of your business."

"Just answer the question."

"Three," his brother admitted and cranked the engine. "Three, okay? I've slept with three women. That doesn't mean I don't know what I want."

"Including Keeley?"

"Including Keeley."

"You don't have enough sexual experience to say Keeley is the one."

"How many women have you slept with?" Linc wheeled from the parking lot.

"A gentleman never kisses and tells."

"A dozen?"

Sebastian laughed.

"Two dozen?"

He couldn't seem to get enough air. He unbuttoned the top button of his shirt and dialed up the air-conditioning vent, turning it up as high as it would go. "My sexual history isn't the issue here. Rather your lack of one."

Linc guided the Toyota onto the expressway and began maneuvering over into the HOV lane. "I prefer quality over quantity."

"Who says I don't have both?"

"I'm not talking about sex. I'm talking about emotional intimacy."

"You sound like a girl." Sebastian hooted. "I mean come on, emotional intimacy?"

"When was the last time you had a serious girlfriend? Oh, wait, you've never had a serious girlfriend."

"Hello." Sebastian spread his arms. "Happy playing the field. And that's exactly what you should be doing."

"With all due respect, Sebastian, I don't think you're the best person to be giving me relationship advice."

Sebastian felt a twinge of something odd in the secret corners of his heart, in a place he didn't want to examine too closely. Linc had been little more than a kid when he'd joined the army after two years of college. The whole time he was overseas Sebastian kept thinking about the day when his brother would come home. He'd imagined them out on the town together, having fun, living the bachelor lifestyle. He'd mentally planned road trips and adventure vacations. He'd envisioned Linc coming to work for him at the PR firm he'd started with nothing but his self-confidence, winning smile and glib tongue.

And while Linc *had* come to work for him, they'd never really had a chance to cut loose, party together or take the trips he'd planned. Keeley had seen to that.

You're jealous.

Sebastian frowned as Linc turned onto the airport road and got into the lane leading to the terminal. Of course he wasn't jealous. What the hell did he have to be jealous of?

He certainly didn't want what Linc had. A bossy woman leading him around by the nose. He'd known for a long time that he wasn't cut out for marriage. He liked his freedom too much.

He had it all. Successful business, big house in Beverly Hills, lots of money in the bank and a little black book filled with names of beautiful, high-profile women.

What more could a man ask for?

"Why are you so afraid of commitment?" Linc asked. "Considering our childhood, and the way your father treated you, I'd think you'd be hungry to find that one special woman to share your life."

"I'm not afraid of commitment." Sebastian reached up and yanked off his tie. He inhaled. Ahh. Getting that noose from around his neck made it easier to breathe.

Linc laughed.

"What?"

"You're terrified."

"I'm not afraid and besides, there is no such thing as one special woman. All women are special."

"Spoken like a man who's never been in love."

That statement irritated Sebastian. What was it about people in love? They turned so smug, as if they'd discovered the ancient secret of the ages or something.

Linc pulled to the curb.

This was it. Time to tell him he was making him a partner. Maybe that would change Linc's mind about this whole marriage nonsense. Sebastian reached into the backseat, unzipped his suitcase and took out the nameplate Blanche had wrapped in gold foil and tied with colored raffia.

Feeling awkward and far too sentimental for his own liking, he thrust the package at Linc. "This is for you."

"What is it?"

"Just open it."

Linc opened the package, then read the lettering out loud. "'Lincoln Holt, partner.'"

Sebastian cocked a grin at his younger brother, smiling past the constriction in his throat. "I promised I'd make you partner."

"Aw, hell, Seb."

"Well?"

Silence filled the car.

"What do you say, partner?"

"Sebastian…there's something else I gotta tell you."

"Keeley's pregnant?" he guessed. It was the only reason he could see for his brother's hasty marriage.

"No, Keeley's not pregnant."

"Did I mention a raise comes with the partnership?"

Linc shook his head. "I can't. Keeley's uncle offered me a position at his security firm in Anaheim and I've accepted."

"Oh?" Sebastian said lightly, as if he didn't care, but inside his gut balled up tight against his spine. "You're jumping ship right after I make you partner?"

Linc met his gaze. "You and I both know that I'm not cut out for public relations and this job with Keeley's uncle would make use of the expertise I gained in the military."

Sebastian felt the same way he did when Linc had told him he'd enlisted, like he'd been kicked in the gut with steel cleats. But he refused to let it show. He gave his brother his best public-relations smile. "This is really what you want?"

"It is." Linc handed him back the nameplate.

He stuffed the damnable thing into his jacket pocket. "Then go for it."

Relief shone in Linc's eyes. "Thanks, man. I appreciate your understanding."

His nose burned. The nameplate weighed heavily in his pocket. He blinked and shrugged. "Not a problem."

Sebastian retrieved his carry-on luggage and humped it into the terminal with a backward wave at his brother. Once he was out of his Linc's sight, he ditched the nameplate in a trash can, straightened his shoulders and moved through the security checkpoint. He found his gate and then boarded the plane, all the while managing not to feel a damned thing.

It was only when they were airborne and he had the Confidential Rejuvenations file in front of him that the familiar—but unwelcome—sensation of abandonment stole over Sebastian.

Knock it off, Black. Stop feeling sorry for yourself. Focus on the job. It always saves your ass.

Work and a night on the town with a beautiful woman.

That was exactly the antidote he needed. It never failed. A new assignment in a new city and a new woman to make him forget all about these unwanted feelings of missing out on something important. He was on the road again and as soon as he got to Austin, he planned on seducing the first appropriate female who crossed his path.

After all, it had been months since he'd had a soft, willing woman in his arms and he had a reputation to uphold.

"DEMARCO," Maxine Woodbury called down the immaculately clean corridor. She was a sixty-nine-year-old emergency-room ward secretary who'd been floated up to Confidential Rejuvenations' sexual dysfunction unit while the regular ward secretary was on maternity leave.

"Yes?"

"You've got a new admit coming in."

Julie DeMarco, R.N., suppressed a heavy sigh. It was her third admission of the day and while that was nothing unusual, the double whammy of crappy news she'd gotten in the morning mail had her feeling far less than her customary enthusiastic self.

Normally, Julie was known around the hospital for her cheery, glass-half-full optimism. She prized a sense of wonder and tried to look at the world with kindness, hope and empathy. Sure, she got teased for it. And yes, she'd been a cheerleader in high school. She couldn't seem to help herself. She did tend to look on the bright side of life.

At work, she favored special-order pink scrubs patterned with red hearts and wore her long, wavy blond hair pulled back in a perky ponytail. Outside of the hospital environment, Julie wore floral prints and paisleys and richly textured fabrics that flowed softly when she moved and she allowed her hair to tumble about her shoulders in unbound curls.

She knew she wasn't a classic beauty. Her eyes were too wide, her forehead a bit too narrow, her lips too lavish and she was self-conscious about her slightly crooked front tooth. She'd promised herself veneers when she'd passed her credentials to become a certified sex therapist, but it looked like the veneers would have to wait. One of the letters she'd received that morning was the disheartening news she'd flunked her qualifying exam.

The second unsettling piece of mail had come from her ex-lover, Roger.

At the thought of the letter resting in the pocket of her lab jacket, Julie curled her fingernails into her palms. Just when she thought she was finally getting over him, he'd sent her into an emotional tailspin again.

Dearest Julie,

These last six months have been torture without you. I think of you constantly and dream of being with you again. I miss the taste of your lips. The sweet lavender scent of your hair. The bright hopefulness of your smile. I would love to get together and rekindle our old bond. Please know you're never far from my thoughts.

All my love,

Roger

The rat bastard wanted a booty call.

She inhaled sharply. His letter held not a single mention of the reason they'd broken up. Julie had discovered that he'd neglected to tell her one crucial little detail about his life.

Roger had a wife. And he had a daughter just eight years younger than she.

It's what you get for dating older men.

The familiar guilt that had haunted her from the day she'd discovered Roger was a married man—the same day she'd broken things off with him—clamped down on her.

She felt like such a stupid romantic fool. Roger had been only her second lover. Her first lover had been her college biology professor, who'd broken up with her once the semester was over and gone on to another student.

She was a walking cliché. Burned twice by older men and her sexual naïveté. Her lack of in-depth, hands-on sexual experience was the main reason she'd asked to be assigned to the sexual dysfunction unit and it was the motivation for her decision to get certified as a sex therapist. She thought the knowledge could help her learn how to differentiate sex from love.

It was something she clearly had trouble doing.

Julie thought about Roger's letter and how much he'd hurt her. She'd been so ashamed she hadn't told anyone about her mistake except her two best friends, Elle and Vanessa.

Her stomach knotted. Until Roger, she'd believed in fairy-tale romances and she'd always thought of herself as a "good" girl. Now she felt tainted, dirty.

Shaking her head, Julie sidled up to the resplendent green granite counter of the nurses' station. "What's the new admit's diagnosis?"

Maxine was a thin, feisty woman who loved Confidential Rejuvenations so much she ignored the fact that she was past retirement age and just kept working. She dyed her hair flame-red and had a penchant for turquoise jewelry. Today she wore a pair of dangly phoenix earrings.

"Priapism." Maxine winked.

This time Julie did sigh. "Priapism" was the medical term for an erection that wouldn't abate even with repeated sexual activity. The cause was usually drug-induced. "Viagra?"

"Some herbal thing."

"Guest's age?"

Confidential Rejuvenations' new policy was to call the patients "guests" as part of the hospital's attempts to revamp their image damaged by recent scandals. In Julie's estimation it was a silly idea, but no one had asked her opinion.

"He's thirty-one."

"So this was a recreational thing, not a home remedy for impotence?"

"Apparently."

Julie frowned. "Boys and their toys."

Maxine glanced over her right shoulder, and then over her left. Finally she leaned forward and lowered her voice. "The patient is a Hollywood director who's been shooting a film here in Austin. He's being admitted under a generic alias to the Corona Suite."

It wasn't uncommon for celebrities to dodge the paparazzi by signing in with bland monikers like Smith or Jones or Black.

"But before you escort him to his suite," Maxine continued, "Dr. Carpenter wants you to put him in exam room one, do a physical assessment and then call him when you're done."

"Gotcha." Julie grabbed her laptop computer that was docked on a rolling cart, and headed off down the tiled corridor to check on the rest of her "guests" before the hotshot Hollywood director showed up on the floor.

She'd just completed her rounds when a man in a beige London Fog raincoat got off the elevator and came toward her. He smelled of musky autumn rain and dark truffles.

Stunned, she stood there staring.

He was movie-star gorgeous, causing her to wonder why he'd chosen a career behind the camera instead of in front of it. Tall and lean, but muscular as an athlete. His thick black hair was brushed back off his forehead, giving him a powerful appearance, which was complemented by his perfectly tailored navy blue suit, cream-colored shirt and maroon silk tie. His eyes were enigmatic, his cheekbones high and chiseled, his mouth wide and inviting. His eyes, fringed by lush lashes, looked black as ink and full of mystery.

He was the kind of man who made even a die-hard romantic like Julie surrender her happily-ever-after daydreams for the promise of one unforgettable night in his bed.

Definitely a Hollywood type. This had to be her guy.

The air between them weighed heavy with expectation. He looked as if he owned the entire hospital and everyone in it. He looked as if he wanted to own her as well.

Feeling ambushed by this totally unexpected and wholly inappropriate sexual attraction, Julie's stomach pitched as a dozen wayward fantasies flipped through her mind.

She pictured herself rolling around on a bearskin rug in a woodsy Alaskan cabin with the guy. She imagined their sweat-drenched bodies pressed together as they made love on the white sand beach in the Canary Islands. She envisioned them writhing against each other on the dance floor of a trendy salsa club as they danced the Lambada.

He was an Artic explorer and she was a native woman offering him the comfort of her igloo…and her body. She was a high-class call girl and he was her frisky sugar daddy and they were joining the mile-high club on a first-class trip to Paris. He was a virile cowboy and she was a sassy saloon gal.

In her wildly imaginative mind, she could taste the briny flavor of his skin as she licked his bare nipple. She inhaled the intrinsic scent of lusty man. She could hear his deep-throated groan as he called out her name in pleasure.

Whoa!

What was wrong with her? He was a patient. She was a nurse. It was inappropriate, unprofessional and wrong on about ten different levels. She should not be feeling these sensations.

And yet, she was.

Stop this now.

She tried to make her mind blank. Tried to tamp down the erotic vision of what his hot male body would look like stripped of his London Fog raincoat and designer suit. She tried to slam the brakes on her taboo fantasies.

But she could not.

Oh, this was bad, bad, bad. She was supposed to be the sex expert, but *she* was the one who needed therapy.

Shocked by the intensity of her emotions, her gaze dropped helplessly to his crotch.

2

SEBASTIAN, who didn't miss a trick, noticed where the nurse's gaze went and he suppressed a smile. "Hi, I'm Mr. Black."

"I've been waiting for you," she murmured.

Oh, no, whispered his impudent ego, *where have you been all my life?* A sexually confident woman bold enough to overtly check out his package in public? He gave her the once-over and the first thing he noticed was that she wasn't wear a wedding band.

Hmm.

Her tongue flicked out and she ran it across her full, strawberry-colored lips.

Spellbound, he simply stared. He liked her. He liked her a lot.

She stood at the end of the corridor in front of a floor-to-ceiling stained glass window. The late-afternoon sun filtering in through the myriad of colors cast a radiant rainbow over her smooth, creamy skin. The center of the stained glass art was an unfurling red rose. The sunlight shimmered, bathing her honey-blond hair, which was pulled back so appealingly in a long ponytail, in a blushing pink glow.

Like zinfandel. Sweet, light, innocent.

The sight was evocative enough to cause instant sweat

to bead on his brow in spite of the temperate climate inside the hospital.

Sebastian had an almost irresistible urge to pull the clasp from her hair and run his fingers through those silky locks. He couldn't pry his eyes off her and he had no idea why. He normally went for leggy redheads with big boobs, not diminutive waifs with vulnerable eyes. His heart literally skipped a beat and the unexpected reaction disturbed him. Usually the only time his pulse skittered was when he successfully steered a client's reputation out of the skids.

His gaze dropped to the round curve of her breasts. Her name tag said *Julie.* A sweet romantic name.

He glanced up.

Their gazes met.

Cemented.

She possessed the most interesting blue eyes he'd ever seen. Eyes the same color of the Pacific Ocean.

Her lips parted.

Sebastian gulped.

Quickly, she glanced away, but then a second later her gaze was on his again, assessing him with slow, deliberate intent until he began to feel like a bug under a microscope.

She narrowed her eyes, pressed her lips together in a firm line and crooked a finger at him. "Come with me."

He followed. At this point, he would have gone straight to hell if that's where she was leading.

Her rubber-soled shoes squeaked quietly against the marble tile. The lemony smell of cleaning solution filled the air. His gaze fixated on the sway of her spectacular ass.

She took a key from her pocket, unlocked a heavy oak door, turned the handle and pushed inside. He went in with her and found himself standing in a state-of-the-art examination room. The leather exam table was obviously new and covered with crisp white butcher paper. The fixtures on the walls were shiny, polished chrome.

Was this where he'd be taking his meeting with the hospital's owners? Unexpected, but okay. Or maybe she was just putting him in here while she went to round up the Confidential Rejuvenations executives.

He shrugged out of his raincoat and hung it on the coatrack beside the door. The room was bigger than a run-of-the-mill exam room, but still small. He turned and found himself face-to-face with her.

She stole his breath with a reassuring smile. The woman made him think of sunflowers and golden retriever puppies and hand-squeezed lemonade. Not a combo he'd ordinarily think of as sensual, but somehow she made wholesome look hot.

Sebastian was acutely aware of a steady strumming of sexual energy flowing from him to her and back again. Her impact was not the full-on whammy of a classic beauty, but instead it was more like the comforting appeal of hot chocolate with miniature marshmallows on an icy winter's day.

You're from L.A., what do you know about an icy winter's day?

Ah, there was the voice of reason struggling to break through the odd spell she'd cast over him. She possessed a certain earthy quality that called to something deep inside him. Something basic, raw and entirely new.

His pulse accelerated. Amazed by his body's overt reaction, Sebastian had to clear his throat in order to speak. "I want…" Dammit, how could he think with her staring at him that way?

"Yes?" she coaxed, low-voiced as a priest in confessional.

I want. I want. I want.

What did he want? Sebastian frowned, yanked his gaze from her sweet lips and looked deeply into her blue eyes, fringed with long lashes. "Uh…"

Terrific, Black, a speechless spin doctor? He couldn't ever recall a woman leaving him tongue-tied.

"Why don't you go ahead and take your clothes off?"

"Huh?" For one wild, incomprehensible moment, he thought she was suggesting they get naked together.

She reached for a pair of purple latex examination gloves resting on the green granite countertop. "I need for you to get undressed so I can do an initial assessment on you and report my findings to Dr. Carpenter."

He blew out a breath of air on a tense laugh. "Oh, no, no, there's been some kind of mix-up."

"There's no need to be ashamed. Many men experience erectile dysfunction."

"Hey, hey, hey. I do *not* have erectile dysfunction."

"Then why were you taking sexual enhancement supplements? Because you know, using impotency drugs—even when it's an herbal medication—simply for fun and games can be deadly for your sexual health."

"Huh?"

"How long have you had the erection?" Her gaze drifted down the length of his body.

He felt the heat of her glance straight to his bones. "Wait, wait." He held up his palms. "You've obviously got me confused with someone else."

At least this explained why she'd been staring at his crotch. Just the thought of having her examine him with those latex gloves on her lithe fingers shot chills up his spine. He didn't know if they were chills of dread or anticipation. The prospect was oddly erotic, but in a scary kind of way.

"You're Mr. Black, correct?"

"Yes, but I'm not a patient."

She frowned. "You're not the movie producer?"

"No."

Flustered, her cheeks pinked and she took a step back, fingering the stethoscope around her neck.

"I'm Sebastian Black, from Back in Black Public Relations. The hospital's hired me to improve Confidential Rejuvenations' image after some recent…er…trouble."

"Oh." Embarrassment deepened the color in her cheeks from pink to red, pushing it all the way into her hairline. "Oh, no."

He smiled to reassure her. "Don't feel sheepish. I should have told you right away why I was here."

"Well…um…I…" Clearly flustered, she dropped her gaze and started for the door, but he was standing in her way.

She went right.

He followed.

Head down, she dodged left.

He beat her to the punch, smoothly blocking her path.

"What?" she demanded, sounding irritated.

"Look at me."

He could tell she didn't want to do it, but he wasn't moving until she did. She tilted her head.

Their gazes met and a renewed voltage surged between them.

He hadn't felt an attraction this potent in a long time. The chemistry both unsettled him and stoked his curiosity. What was it about her that so piqued his interest?

It's not about her. You're just susceptible because of what happened this morning with Linc.

"It was a natural mistake," he soothed.

"You don't have to spin it for me," she said, surprising him by recognizing what he was doing. "Let's tell the truth. I made an idiot out of myself by not asking what was the nature of your business the minute you arrived."

"You were trying to spare me humiliation. You thought I had been playing around with some Viagra kind of thing and got myself into trouble."

"You're too smooth for my own good," she said. "You ought to come with a warning label. Something along the lines of 'Warning—man may appear more charming than he really is.'"

"How do you know I'm not as charming as I appear?" He grinned, enjoying their sparring.

She tossed her head and her ponytail bounced pertly. "I've had dealings with charming men before."

He arched an eyebrow. "You don't say."

"To my detriment, I might add."

Sebastian took a wild guess. "A charming man left you brokenhearted?"

"Something like that." She brushed a strand of hair from her eyes. "Anyway, I learned my lesson. Now, if you'll excuse me, Mr. Black, I have to find my real patient."

"The guy with the irrepressible boner?"

"Mr. Black," she scolded, but her eyes were lively. "That's inappropriate."

"You're right—" he flicked his gaze to her name tag "—Julie."

"It's Miss DeMarco."

"Miss? As in not married?" His eyes drifted to the bare ring finger of her left hand. He might play the field, but as far as he knew, Sebastian had never bedded a married woman and he wasn't about to start.

"As in none of your business. Now if you'll get out of my way, I'd appreciate it."

He'd pushed too far. Sebastian was smart enough to know when to back off. He stepped aside and she brushed past him on her way out the door.

The contact—their first touching—was nothing short of electrifying.

They both inhaled audibly in a simultaneous breath. She stopped in midstride and their gazes seared again. He felt like a pistol. Hot, cocked and loaded.

She was right. He was inappropriate.

"Look," he said, "we got off on the wrong foot. Why don't we start all over?" He thrust out a hand. "Hello, I'm Sebastian Black."

She hesitated and just when he decided she wasn't about to take his hand, she reached out. "Julie DeMarco."

He grasped her soft palm and she squeezed lightly. His entire arm tingled and he experienced a hot rush of sexual energy surge through every cell in his body and the hairs on the nape of his neck rose to attention.

The sight of their clasped hands riveted him. Her creamy skin was much lighter than his. She was all soft and smooth. He was hard and rough. The contrast in their two hands would have made one hell of a photo. Man, woman. Strength, delicacy. Tanned, pale. United.

A familiar rush of adrenaline. The thrill of the chase. Outside in the hallway, in the silence of his indrawn breath, Sebastian could hear a cart being pushed, wheels squeaking, in need of oil. In that moment Sebastian understood that one way or the other, he was going to take this woman to bed.

"Pleased to meet you, Julie DeMarco."

And then he had a brilliant idea that would effectively kill two birds with one stone. A solution that could help him solve Confidential Rejuvenations' image problem, plus get him closer to the appealing Miss DeMarco. The technique had served him well on many campaigns.

"Listen," he said, "I need your help."

"My help?"

She looked so cute with her brow furrowed and her bottom lip tucked up between her teeth. Good thing she was no longer investigating the zipper of his pants. She'd see that the Viagra abuser wasn't the only one with a boner.

"I need an insider's view."

"An insider's view?"

"To help me see Confidential Rejuvenations in a way only someone who works in the trenches can. I'd like to hear what you think about the recent scandals."

"I can't violate patient confidentiality."

"Nor would I ever ask you to do so." He smiled. "I'd just like to get your take."

"Why me?"

"I need input from several sources, not just the bigwigs in the expensive suits. Let's be honest, they're out of touch with what really goes on behind the scenes."

"Bigwigs in expensive suits like you?"

"Touché." She was feisty. He liked that. "What do you say?"

"I don't know if that would be such a good idea."

"Do you always work the swing shift?"

"Yes."

"Does your shift start at three?"

"Two-thirty."

"How 'bout this. I meet you for lunch at the sushi restaurant down the block that I saw when I was driving in."

"Are you always this pushy, Mr. Black?"

His gaze held hers. "Only when I see something I want."

She made a small noise in the back of her throat and gave him a cool, assessing glance. He noticed the pulse at the hollow of her neck quickened. Ah, just as he suspected. She liked him, whether she was willing to admit it or not.

"So it's a date," he said as a statement, not a question, but his gut squeezed.

Julie pursed her lips, her frown deepening.

She's going to say no. His hopes took the express elevator to his shoes.

What in the hell was the matter with him? Why was he so disappointed at the thought she'd reject him? He hadn't felt this nervous around a woman in years. Blame his aberrant anxiety on the fact his brother had dropped the marriage bomb on him that morning and he was off his game.

It had been too long. He was a bit chagrined to realize he hadn't had sex in almost ten months. Not because he hadn't had plenty of chances, but mainly because no woman had excited him enough to give chase.

But Julie DeMarco had changed all that in record time.

She sank her hands on her hips. He saw the word *no* forming on those full, luscious lips. His disappointment was surprisingly sharp-edged.

She held his gaze.

He heard blood rushing through his ears, felt his body tighten.

"Okay," she murmured. "I'll do it. I'll give you an interview."

"I MET A GUY." Julie grinned at her best friends, Elle Nash and Dr. Vanessa Rodriquez. They were sharing a pitcher of beer at a hole-in-the-wall pizza parlor near the University of Texas, which served up the best deep-dish pie in Austin. For the first time since she'd broken up with Roger, Julie was interested in someone and she simply had to crow about it.

It was almost midnight, but the place didn't close until 2:00 a.m. and it was a handy meeting spot, equal distance from all their homes and Confidential Rejuvenations. Elle and Julie both had worked swing shift that evening and Vanessa had stayed late catching up on backlogged paperwork.

"I'm having lunch with him tomorrow." She was making it sound like a date, but what was wrong with that? Who knew what direction things might take? One thing was clear, they had chemistry.

It's not a date.

Okay, so it wasn't really a date. It was an interview, but still, he'd certainly seemed interested in her. Which was surprising, considering how she'd embarrassed herself over a case of mistaken identity. Remembering what had transpired in the exam room, she bit down on the inside of her cheek.

"A date?" Elle was a sensible redhead with dazzling green eyes and a way of smiling that made everyone like her immediately. She reached for a second slice of pepperoni-and-black-olive pizza. "That's great. It's about time. I'm happy for you."

"Who's the guy?" Vanessa asked over the rim of her frosty beer mug. Vanessa was a beautiful Latina with long black hair, chocolate-brown eyes and a Mensa IQ. "Anyone we know?"

"His name is Sebastian Black."

Vanessa set her mug down and leaned back against the

red vinyl booth. "Is he the public-relations specialist from L.A. that the hospital's board of directors hired to polish Confidential's tarnished image?"

"He is."

"You move fast," Elle said. "He just got in to town. The entire E.R. staff's buzzing about how cute he is."

"He was the fast mover." Julie recalled those tense, exciting moments in the exam room when they'd touched. Her fingers were still tingling from the contact.

"Watch out, Tanner filled me in on the guy's reputation," Vanessa said, referring to her fiancé, Tanner Doyle. As head of security at Confidential Rejuvenations, it was Tanner's job to check the backgrounds of all potential employees, including contract workers. "Sebastian Black may be an excellent spin doctor, but he's also got a reputation as something of a player."

Julie's stomach squeezed. Mindlessly, she pleated the red-and-white-checkered paper napkin in her lap. "Meaning…?"

"Handsome, rich, commitment-phobic. Rumor has it he's got a woman in every city he visits."

"What's wrong with that?" she surprised herself by asking.

Vanessa and Elle gave each other startled looks, then turned to stare at Julie.

"Well?" she asked. "Why are you looking at me like that?"

"You feel her forehead and see if she has a fever," Vanessa told Elle. "I'll check her pulse."

They moved as if they were actually going to do it. Laughing, Julie held up her palms. "I'm not feverish, honest."

Elle picked the olives off her pizza. "Where's our little die-hard romantic? You were the one coaching us not to give up on romance and now, here you are, ready to take up with a playboy who'll only end up breaking your heart."

"About that," Julie said. "I've been thinking..."

"Yes?" Her friends leaned forward, hanging on to her every word.

"Maybe it's time I shook things up a little. Took a walk on the wild side. I've never been very good at separating love from sex and I think maybe it's time I learned. I'm twenty-nine and after the number Roger did on me..." She let her words trail off.

"Seriously?" Elle asked.

Julie glanced over her shoulder to see if anyone was within earshot, then leaned closer to her friends and lowered her voice. "It's been six months since Roger and I'm feeling—"

"Horny?" Vanessa supplied.

"Sexually frustrated." Julie preferred her own word choice. She wasn't as frank and earthy as her friend. "You guys, I think that's why I failed my certifying exam. I've been having erotic dreams lately and I've been so distracted by them I can hardly concentrate on my work."

Vanessa looked at Elle and nodded. "She's horny. That's my official medical diagnosis. Nothing wrong with being horny. It happens. Part of the human condition. Nothing to feel awkward about."

"I don't feel awkward."

Vanessa waved a hand. "How come your face is turning as red as this booth?"

"Okay, all right." Julie took a deep breath. "I'm horny. I need a man. And not just any man. I need a man who's good in bed, but one who is not looking for a relationship. I need a no-strings-attached affair and I need it now."

"Where is this coming from?" Elle asked. "This philosophy is so not you. Not that I think it's a bad idea, mind you. Just that it's not like you."

Julie pulled Roger's letter out of her pocket, unfolded it and passed it to her friend.

Elle read it and then handed Roger's letter to Vanessa. "What a weasel."

"Oh, no, he didn't," Vanessa said after reading it. "The jerk."

"I'm tired of being a starry-eyed romantic," Julie said. "I'm sick of being naive when it comes to men."

"And you think a fling with a totally inappropriate guy will fix that?" Vanessa raised a skeptical eyebrow.

"I know it will."

"What's going to keep you from falling in love with him?" Elle asked.

"His total inappropriateness."

Vanessa dragged another slice of pizza onto her plate. "Being totally inappropriate didn't stop you from falling for Roger."

Julie took a sip of her beer. It had gone warm. She grimaced. "That's because I didn't know he was inappropriate until I found out about his wife."

"And his daughter who's only a few years younger than you," Elle pointed out. "Don't forget."

Julie jammed on a false smile. "Thank you so much for reminding me."

"So you've set your sights on Sebastian Black as your totally inappropriate rebound guy?" Vanessa asked.

Had she? Until this moment, she hadn't realized exactly what she'd been thinking, but yeah, maybe she had.

"It sounds like this Sebastian character is used to

speeding in the fast lane and let's face it, sweetie, you're a slow-lane kinda girl," Vanessa added.

"He did more than turn my head. Sebastian had me so confused I mistook him for a patient." Julie explained about the Hollywood bigwig patient with priapism and Sebastian's appearance on the wrong floor at exactly the wrong time, leading to one of the most embarrassing moments of her life.

The fact that Julie was even considering a temporary fling should have been a huge red flag. For her entire life she'd been the girl who collected housewares and linens for her hope chest and cut out pictures from brides' magazines to paste into her wedding-plan book. Her favorite game had been Mystery Date. She was the girl who plastered posters of boy bands on her wall and kept a pink diary filled with teenage angst about her many crushes.

It hardly seemed fair that her friends had found true love while she was the one who was still single and searching. Not that she resented them their happiness. She just wanted her share, too.

Maybe Vanessa was right. There was no way she was cut out for a bumpy ride in the fast lane. She should probably call up Sebastian and tell him she couldn't meet him for lunch tomorrow.

Where's the harm in lunch? She was being nudged by the part of herself that hungered for excitement and the thrill of something new.

"Jules?" Elle said. "You okay?"

"Huh?" She blinked, realized her friend had said something to her and she hadn't even heard it.

"I don't want to see you get hurt again." Elle put a hand on Julie's arm. "Remember how long it took you to get over Roger?"

Way too long. That was why she needed someone new, someone fresh, someone fun, someone like Sebastian.

She met Elle's gaze. "I do appreciate your concern. I'll be careful. I promise."

Vanessa grinned. "Make sure to pick up some condoms. Ribbed, for your pleasure."

Julie's mouth went dry. Maybe she wasn't up for this after all.

"Please, make sure not to romanticize him. He's just a guy," Elle said.

"Like Dante was just a guy?" Julie asked, referring to Elle's new husband, Dr. Dante Nash, who'd been undercover for the FBI when he'd busted Elle's ex-husband, Mark Lawson.

"That's different," Elle said hastily. "I had to learn how to be romantic. You're trying to learn not to be so romantic. You're the one with unrealistic ideas about love."

True enough. Julie sucked in her breath as she thought about Sebastian. Just remembering his dark, curly hair had her fingers tingling to run through those thick locks. The core of her sex tightened. Her body wanted him, no question about that.

But was she brave enough to step on the accelerator and change lanes? Did she have what it took for a wild, adventuresome fling? Could she really forsake her romantic nature, learn how to have sex for sex's sake and leave love out of the equation?

3

FOLLOWING HIS DINNER meeting with Confidential Rejuvenations' co-owners, Sebastian holed up in the presidential suite Blanche had reserved for him in Austin's most luxurious private hotel. The meeting had gone well, but he felt unaccountably edgy.

After stripping off his suit jacket and tie, he tossed them on the bed, then moved to pull the draperies that revealed a sliding glass door. Sebastian unlatched the lock and stepped out on the balcony that overlooked the Colorado River.

City lights twinkled below. He heard the sound of traffic and somewhere in the distance an outdoor band was playing so loudly the music drifted up to the tenth floor. He caught a whiff of exhaust fumes mingled with the spicy scent of cumin, onions, garlic and chili powder from the hotel's Mexican restaurant.

He leaned over the railing, drummed his fingers on the cool metal and wondered why he was so keyed up.

The feeling was more than his usual fast-paced, get-the-job-done eagerness. There was a strange and new underlying restlessness. He kept thinking about Julie DeMarco and their odd encounter in the Confidential Rejuvenations' exam room. Something about her made him feel…

What?

He couldn't express what he was feeling. He only knew this agitated sensation wasn't normal. Had it started with her? Or did it lead back to this morning when Linc told him he was getting married and leaving the firm?

You're kidding yourself if you think it's just a reaction to Linc's news.

Every time he thought about Julie his insides knotted up. She was small-boned and delicate and ultrafeminine and pretty to a point. But her cheeks were just a little too round to be perfect, her chin a little too sharp. She had a crooked front tooth that shouldn't have been cute, but it was.

No, Julie wasn't the kind of woman who immediately turned male heads when she swayed into a room, but definitely once she smiled, she'd be noticed. She was also the kind of woman that could intimidate most commitment-phobic men simply by blinking those honest big baby blues.

Somehow she'd gotten to him.

Sebastian thought about the promise he'd made himself that morning. He'd vowed to seduce the first appropriate female who crossed his path. Well, Julie was certainly appropriate and he definitely wanted her, yet suddenly, seducing her seemed too cavalier.

Too cruel.

Like hunting Bambi with a bazooka.

You don't have to seduce her. Tomorrow's lunch could simply be lunch. Forget ulterior motives. Just interview her for behind-the-scenes info at Confidential Rejuvenations and let it go at that.

Good advice.

He had to stop thinking about her and the only way to do that was to get to work. It was 9:00 p.m. in Austin, but he was on California time. He stepped back from the balcony, pulled the sliding glass door closed and headed to the briefcase he'd dropped by the front door.

After he took out the Confidential Rejuvenations file, he sank down at the desk chair to flip through it. On top was a slick brochure printed on the finest paper money could buy. It showed the colloquial architecture of the hospital that made it look like a spa resort. That was the general idea—it was a healing center as opposed to a medical facility.

He'd been there in person. The brochure didn't lie. At least not about the appearance of the place. The lush green lawns were perfectly clipped, as were the bountiful privacy hedges. Ivy-twined trellises shaded genteel park benches. The profusion of fall flowers in full bloom testified to the exemplary gardening skills of the groundskeepers. A luxurious flagstone walkway led to the front entrance in one direction, while the other fork winded its way to an elaborate hand-carved gazebo positioned on a bluff above the river's sensuous curve.

What the brochure wisely didn't reveal was beneath the serene surface, behind the healing promises made in the glossy brochure, beyond those quiet vine-covered walls, a shadowy menace lurked. Careers lay on the line. Fortunes stood to be lost. Reputations hung in the balance.

And Sebastian was the fixer. Hired to bring his particular expertise to the situation and work his magic.

Confidential Rejuvenations had been founded in 1993 by Dr. Jarrod Butler and Dr. William Covey and a famous action-movie actor who'd left Hollywood for his native Austin. Ten years later, after a bout with booze and pills, the actor had needed a return on his investment and sold out his share in Confidential Rejuvenations to a greedy young surgeon named Mark Lawson.

Several months ago, Lawson had been murdered by a mobster on the Confidential Rejuvenations' campus in a drug deal gone bad. Not long after that, Texas state senator Robert Garcia had bought Lawson's share in the hospital. Only to have his adopted daughter, Chloe—who'd been a scrub nurse at the facility—try to murder Confidential Rejuvenations' head of security, Tanner Doyle. Although the police had ruled that Lawson's death and the attempt on Doyle's life were not connected to the other occurrences, it remained a PR nightmare.

From the very day Confidential Rejuvenations had opened its doors, there had been rumors, speculation and gossip. It did, after all, cater to the rich and famous. It was a place where the crème de la crème revealed their inner secrets, exposed their vulnerabilities and sought to escape their problems. Unlike most hospitals, Confidential Rejuvenations' specialties were designed to fit the lifestyles of an elite clientele.

Sebastian flipped the page, reading about the services offered. Innovative cosmetic surgery, cutting-edge anti-aging therapy, pioneer treatment in obsessive-compulsive disorders, state-of-the-art substance abuse facilities and revolutionary sexual dysfunction remedies.

Sexual dysfunction.

The unit where Julie DeMarco worked.

He pushed aside that thought and the unexpected sexual stirring that came with it.

After reviewing the entire file and further brushing up on the problems plaguing Confidential Rejuvenations in recent months, he opened his laptop and began compiling a plan of action into the PR software he'd invented.

What he hoped to accomplish was not just information

gathering to spark innovative ideas for his PR campaign, but to snoop around and see if he could discover who was behind the sabotage.

He was just cocky enough to think he might succeed where law enforcement and hospital security had failed. People didn't open up to cops and security guards. On that score, his charm stood him in good stead. He had no trouble coaxing people into spilling their secrets.

Idly, he wondered what secrets Julie DeMarco hid behind those sweet, guileless blue eyes. He'd discovered that everyone had secrets, even the most innocent.

Sebastian was deep in the middle of his media campaign plan when his computer played a snippet from the Bond movie theme song "For Your Eyes Only," letting him know he had an instant message from Blanche.

He flicked a switch and turned on his Internet camera for a video conference. Blanche was sitting at her desk, looking prim and proper in a double-breasted fawn-colored suit, her iron-gray curls perfectly coiffed.

"How's Austin?" she asked.

"Fine. Watcha still doing at the office?"

"Just finishing up. I'm on my way out the door. I thought I'd check on you. See if you needed anything."

"You work too hard."

"Pot. Kettle. Black."

"Ah, but I play just as hard as I work. You don't play, dear Blanche."

Blanche gave him a Mona Lisa smile. "You think you know me so well."

"Come on," he said, suddenly realizing that other than his brother, Blanche was his only real friend. He spent too much time in hotel rooms just like this one. It was pretty sad when you were a thirty-year-old guy and your best friend was a fifty-something grandmother. Maybe he did work too hard. "If you had a social life you wouldn't be at the office at eight at night."

"You don't know what I'm doing here. Perhaps I have a suitor and I'm showing him my desk."

"Are you?" Sebastian lifted an eyebrow.

"I'll never tell."

"So what's up?"

"I just wanted to make sure you were all right. Linc told me he's quitting and that he and Keeley are getting married. How do you feel about that?"

Sebastian shrugged. "I feel fine."

"Liar."

"Okay, you want the truth? I think Linc's making a big mistake," he said.

"He loves her. She loves him."

"They're wrong for each other."

"How do you know?"

"They're total opposites."

"Opposites attract."

He thought of Julie, laughed and shook his head.

"Oh," Blanche said. "I see."

"See what?"

"What's her name?"

"Her? What are you talking about?"

"You're already penning another new name in your little black book."

"I'm not," he denied, wondering how in the hell Blanche knew him so well.

She tilted her head. "You're working on it."

"What can I say," he confessed. "I love women."

Sebastian did love women. They fascinated him. With their potions and perfumes that smelled so good. From their soft skin, to the delicate underside of their throats. And the way their minds worked, so mysterious and unpredictable.

The opposite sex mesmerized him. Tall ones, short ones, plump ones, thin ones, dark ones, light ones. He loved them all. It was the reason he couldn't choose just one. There were simply too many wonderful ladies walking about the world.

"Maybe you should consider backing off," Blanche said.

"What?"

"You rush into courtships."

Courtships? He grinned. Blanche was so old-fashioned. He found it endearing. "Hey, I'm usually only in town a short time. If I didn't rush, I wouldn't get anywhere."

"And then just as quickly, you rush out of them. You'll never get married like that."

"You know I'm not interested in marriage."

"I know you *say* you're not interested in marriage," Blanche said. "I think it's that you haven't met the right woman. When you do, everything will change and then you'll finally understand about your brother and Keeley."

The truth was he didn't want to understand. "Yeah? Well, if you know so much about men and women and love, how come you're single?"

Blanche straightened in her chair, making herself look even more prim than usual. "I've had my great love affair, Sebastian. No one else could ever compare to Edward, so there's no point searching. He's gone. I'm a grandmother, which keeps me happy enough, and I've got you to look after."

"Now see," Sebastian said. "If I did something stupid like fall in love and get married, then you wouldn't have anyone to take care of. How could I ever do that to you?"

Blanche's opinion came out in a snort. He'd gotten quite accustomed to the expressive sound and it made him smile. "Good night, Sebastian. Call me if you need anything."

"Sleep tight, Blanche."

She turned off her computer camera and that was the end of the conversation. Sebastian finished up his work and logged off. He kicked off his shoes and flopped onto the bed, hands cupped behind his head. His thoughts trailed to Julie.

He couldn't figure out what it was about her that appealed to him so much. She was cute, sure. And he loved her curvy, compact body. Just thinking about touching her had him growing hard. He wanted her…oh, yeah.

But he had a nagging feeling she was a forever kind of woman and that simply wasn't what he was looking for. He thought about calling her up, canceling their luncheon appointment, but then he realized it was almost midnight.

Why was he so confused about what he wanted from her? He was normally very decisive. In that exam room he'd decided he was going to seduce her. But after talking to Blanche, he was feeling…

What was he feeling?

Sebastian pushed the thought away. Blanche loved messing with his head. He wasn't going to let her get to him. He did know what he wanted and he was going after it.

A nice little fling with Julie DeMarco.

SO THEY THOUGHT they could hire a spin doctor to solve Confidential Rejuvenations' image problems, eh?

Fools.

The hospital saboteur rummaged through the file on the cocky Mr. Sebastian Black. He was a good-looking devil. No question about it. With his lush dark hair and straight white teeth. Veneers, no doubt.

And from the curriculum vitae the saboteur had found on Dr. Butler's desk, Sebastian Black ran one of the most sought-after, privately owned PR firms in the country. His clients included important movers and shakers in the entertainment industry.

Mr. Black, the saboteur had discovered, had quite a reputation as a ladies' man. The saboteur chuckled. Such a man would be so easy to manipulate.

What a wickedly wonderful turn of events that he was interested in Julie DeMarco.

That woman needed to be taught a lesson. Shamelessly sleeping with a married man. Was nothing sacred anymore? DeMarco deserved to get her heart broken by a notorious playboy like Black and the saboteur was in a special position to make that heartbreak happen.

The plan was brilliant. Use public relations to turn the tables on the PR expert. Anticipation—and revenge—was a glorious dish to be savored.

JULIE WAS SO NERVOUS she could scarcely breathe. She hadn't been on a date since she'd sent Roger packing.

It's not a date, she told herself. It's an interview in a public place. There will be lots of people around.

Moistening her lips to quell her nervousness, Julie sat in her white Honda Civic outside the Sushi Palace a half mile from Confidential Rejuvenations. She was early. It was only eleven-forty but she'd been too keyed up to stay at home.

Her shift started at two-thirty and she had her scrubs folded in the backseat, along with her pink nursing clogs and a pink stethoscope. It would have been more convenient to meet him already dressed in her scrub uniform, but Julie wanted Sebastian to see what she looked like in street clothes.

She'd spent almost an hour getting ready. The entire time, she'd kept asking herself whether Sebastian Black was really the rebound guy she wanted after Roger. Or, if she was being honest with herself, could she admit he was really too much for her to handle?

That was the question she was here to answer.

After a phone consultation with Vanessa and Elle, she'd dressed sexily, but not too vampish, considering it was a luncheon date. Straight-legged black slacks, black zippered fashion boots with three-inch heels to give her five-foot-three stature a boost and a pink-and-white-striped angora sweater. She used her curling iron on her hair and it hung low down her back in soft, feminine ringlets.

This was exactly what she needed—a temporary tryst with a man who knew his way around a woman's body. A man who could take the lead and teach her what she needed to know.

That was her secret. When it came to sex, she really didn't know what she was doing. Failing her qualifying exam to become a sex therapist was proof enough of her inadequacies.

Before Roger, she'd had only one other lover—her college biology professor, Phillip Gregory. She'd given him her virginity and he'd given her an A-plus for the semester and then he'd dumped her. Phillip had broken her nineteen-year-old heart and damaged her self-esteem, but she'd never stopped looking for love.

Now, she was almost thirty years old and she could count on both hands the number of times she'd had sex. Three times with Phillip. Seven times with Roger.

Pathetic.

It was this damned starry-eyed romanticism instilled in her by her mother. The promise of happily-ever-after. The dream of the one perfect guy who made your life complete. Her mother had believed it and look where it had gotten her. Married to her soul mate, but then widowed at fifty-four with a teenage daughter to raise.

Julie had to ask herself if that's why she'd been attracted to both Roger and Phillip. Had she simply been searching for a father figure? Her dad had died when she was fourteen. Had her lovers represented the masculine guidance she'd lost and longed for?

What a cliché.

Julie peered at herself in the rearview mirror and was startled to see how sexy she looked. Her curls had defied the curling iron and resorted to their usual wild tumble, giving her a just-rolled-out-of-bed appearance. Suddenly, her lipstick seemed too red, her mascara too thickly applied, the V-neck of her sweater revealing too much cleavage.

Well, that was the point, wasn't it? To start something with Sebastian Black. Learn a few tricks. Push her sexual boundaries with a no-strings-attached affair? Get past the number Roger and Phillip had done on her self-confidence. Become more accomplished at lovemaking so she didn't get so embarrassed in therapy sessions when the patients revealed their colorful romantic escapades.

Nervously, she drummed her fingers on the steering wheel. What was she doing here? What made her think Sebastian Black could cure her romanticism?

A zippy red sports car pulled into the parking lot and she knew before she ever saw his face that Sebastian was behind the wheel. He killed the engine and hopped from the low-slung German-engineered automobile looking as if he'd stepped off the cover of *People* magazine. Tall, broad shouldered, lean hipped. Sexy as hell.

You're in over your head. This guy will eat you alive.

It was, she had to admit, a very delicious thought.

Sebastian clutched a black leather briefcase in his hand and he headed for the door of the restaurant with purposeful, ground-chewing strides. He wore a tailor-made gray business suit with a lavender shirt and an avant-garde grape-and-gold tie. Not many men could pull off lavender, but on him, it was a power color, accenting his tanned skin and dark, intelligent eyes. Modern young executive on the go.

He was exquisite.

And he was everything she'd trained herself not to want. Handsome beyond belief. Smooth as silk. The kind of guy you just knew would take your breath away and leave you gasping for oxygen. She'd always gone for substance over style. For older steady men who promised security.

Yeah. And look where that got you.

It was all she could do to keep from starting her car, driving away and thanking her lucky stars she'd escaped unscathed.

But despite her alarm, something pushed her forward. Her craving for knowledge and sexual experimentation was stronger than her fear of getting hurt. She could do this. She could seduce him, enjoy him and keep the relationship strictly casual. He was only in town for a short time. He was perfect.

She put her hand on the door handle, opened it and stepped out into the parking lot. Sebastian had already gone inside. Determined, she headed into the restaurant.

The hostess, a pretty, dark-haired woman in a red kimono with green dragons imprinted into the silk fabric, greeted her in the foyer. "One for lunch?"

"Actually," she said, "I'm meeting someone."

Just then, Sebastian walked up behind the hostess. He'd been watching for her. His grin widened as if he'd just won the Powerball lottery. The eager expression on his face went a long way toward bolstering her courage and tamping down her fear.

He made a low noise of masculine appreciation as he came closer. "Wow, check you out."

Slowly, he raked his gaze from the top of her head, down the low-cut V of her angora sweater, to the snug-fitting, straight-legged slacks to her high-heeled black stiletto boots and back again. The look was so intense, Julie gulped and folded her fingernails into her palms to steady her nerves.

An electrical charge passed between them. A silent understanding. His dark eyes smoldered with a sexuality that stole her breath.

He was unfairly handsome. No guy should look so good. It was annoying that every female in the place was darting surreptitious glances in his direction.

To his credit, his focus was only on her. He made her feel special and that made her suspicious. Why was he trying so hard?

Julie inhaled sharply, desperate for air.

Sebastian extended his hand.

The moment their palms touched the hostess disappeared. The restaurant ceased to exist. Time evaporated. She was aware of nothing except Sebastian. No man had ever looked at her in quite that way before.

Oh, he's good.

He was very, very good at making her feel special. Julie told herself it was his job. He was a PR expert. It wasn't personal. She would not let it go to her head.

Old habits died hard. She was a natural-born romantic and going against her tendencies would not come easy.

He dropped her hand at last and the spell was broken.

She inhaled raggedly, her gaze still welded to his. Every hair on his head was in place. He wore his tailored suit as if it was an extension of his body. He had the most gorgeous mouth. Full, but not too big. She licked her own lips.

"You ready to get down to business?"

She blinked. "Huh?"

"The interview?"

"Oh, yes. Absolutely." She tapped her forehead. "Anything you need."

"Anything?" He grinned rakishly and his gaze took another trip over the length of her body.

Don't blush, don't blush.

Too late. Her cheeks heated.

Terrific. She was blushing. Giving herself away. Why did she have to be so fair? Why couldn't she have taken after her father's side of the family, with his Italian heritage, instead of her Swedish mother?

"Our table is this way." With a proprietary touch that both excited and bothered her, he took her elbow and guided her to the back of the restaurant.

Her heart rate soared as she caught a whiff of his scent. He smelled of cool sage and a startling twist of hot nutmeg. She had an urge to nibble the flesh of his earlobe and see if he tasted as good as he smelled.

A physical reaction ignited inside her. It was as if all her glands—pineal, adrenal, pituitary, parotid—were functioning overtime, all secreting at maximum capacity. Saliva filled her mouth. Epinephrine sped through her bloodstream. Heat suffused her pelvis. She was a walking chemistry lab.

The sudden desire unsettled her. This wicked lick of unexpected sensory pleasure.

There were no other diners in their immediate area. A nosegay of purple and peach orchids rested in the center of the table and she was surprised to see a card beside the flowers with her name on them.

"The flowers are for me?"

"To thank you," he said. "For agreeing to let me interview you. Go ahead. Open the card."

Her fingers were damp against the matte finish of the envelope. She slipped the note out.

To ensure you never confuse me with anyone else again,
Sebastian.

She didn't have the courage to look at him directly. "The flowers weren't necessary."

"You don't like them."

"I'm overwhelmed. How did you know they're my favorite flowers and my favorite colors?"

"I asked around."

The fact he'd taken the time to ask around about her was flattering. "Th-thank you," she stammered.

"You're welcome." He pulled her chair out for her. His warm breath feathered the hairs along the nape of her neck. She tried not to be impressed with his courtly manners. He knew all the tricks to set a woman's heart pattering.

Careful.

Her self-esteem couldn't survive another mistake courtesy of the male species.

He stepped away and sat down in the chair next to her.

To distract herself she unfurled the white linen napkin

that was wrapped around her silverware and settled it into her lap. Julie observed him through lowered lashes, shyly issuing him a provocative invitation with her eyes. She wasn't much good at flirting and she hoped she was pulling this off.

He angled his head. The way he looked at her made her feel so beautiful. She wasn't accustomed to so easily capturing a man's rapt attention. Especially a man like him.

She had the oddest sensation that if she didn't look away now, she would forever be melded to him. She cleared her throat, smoothed her napkin in her lap. "Fire when ready."

"Pardon."

"Your questions. The interview."

"Right, the interview." Sebastian shifted, leaned closer. His smile was so damned distracting. "How long have you worked at Confidential Rejuvenations?"

"It's the only job I've ever had. I started right out of nursing school. My friend Elle told me they had openings."

"And you've always worked on the sexual dysfunction unit?"

"Oh, no." She shook her head. "I started there only a few months ago. Before that, I worked in newborn nursery."

"Why the switch?"

She wasn't about to tell him she'd changed positions because she felt the need to overcome her lack of sexual sophistication. She was embarrassed enough as it was. She could still remember Roger teasing her because she hadn't known how to give a blow job.

"I get the impression the specialty isn't a good fit for you."

"Why do you say that?" she asked, feeling irritated.

"I don't know." He shrugged. "I bet there's a lot of dark

and kinky things that get revealed on a unit specializing in sexual dysfunction and you seem like such a sweet and wholesome woman."

"Well, I'm not," she snapped.

He had a smart-ass look on his face that said *sure you're not.*

"And even if I were sweet and wholesome, which I'm not, don't you think that people having a sexual crisis need someone to look up to? Someone who can act as a role model?"

"They need someone who's been there. Someone who understands what they're going through. Someone who knows what it's like to be swept away by temptations they can't control," Sebastian said.

He was right and she knew it. Damn him.

"I understand," she lied.

"Yeah?"

She raised her chin. "Yes."

"So you wouldn't be upset if I did this?"

Julie started to ask what he meant, but she didn't get any further than "Did wh—" before Sebastian's mouth closed over hers.

4

SEBASTIAN REALLY hadn't meant to kiss her. He'd just wanted to call her bluff, but somehow, he'd been unable to stop himself from leaning across the table and planting his mouth over hers.

Damn if she didn't taste as good as she looked.

And she surprised him by eagerly kissing him back. That wasn't all. The desperate hunger shooting through his body shocked him as well. He was attracted to her, yes. But he'd never felt anything quite like this.

What did it mean?

He almost pulled away. Almost stopped the kiss right then and there.

But she was having none of it. Her arms went around his neck. Her lips parted and her sweet, warm tongue came out to play. To tell the truth, she freaked him out a little.

She caught him off guard. He had not pegged her as being sexually responsive, especially in a public place. But he, of all people, should know that you couldn't judge what was inside a package from the pretty wrapping paper.

He cupped her head in the palms of his hands, pushed his fingers through her hair and fisted them. She didn't flinch at his roughness. He wasn't usually rough, but she brought out the animal in him.

He fell into her rhythm. Just tumbled. He kissed her so hard he could taste her on the back of his throat. She met his demanding kiss, slipping her tongue as far into his mouth as it would go. She kissed him as if she knew all his secrets, all his flaws, all his missteps, and she liked him anyway.

The knowledge floored him.

God, but she was one hell of a woman. He breathed her in. She smelled of vanilla-scented soap and bright autumn sunshine. Sweet, yet as vibrant as the change of seasons.

Her attractiveness went much deeper than surface allure. Sure she was pretty but it wasn't what captivated him. He was equally attracted to her odd mix of shyness and sass. Her unexpected daring coupled with that cute little blush snatched up his imagination and refused to let go. Her charm was genuine, seeded within her flesh, her bones, her very breath.

She was fresh and surprising and interesting. And he couldn't stop wanting to run his hands over ever inch of her body. He couldn't stop tasting the richness of her sweet, potent mouth. Couldn't stop his cock from turning to granite.

Then abruptly, she broke off the kiss, slumped back in her chair. Her eyes were wide and she was breathing heavily.

Everyone in the restaurant was staring at them. He supposed they must have caused quite a spectacle with their kiss. He hesitated a moment, not knowing what to do. Julie gazed up at him as if he was some kind of chest-thumping caveman.

"I apologize," he heard himself mumble. "I crossed the line."

She kept studying him as if he was a complex jigsaw puzzle.

"I shouldn't have acted on my instincts. I wanted to kiss you, so I did, but that was inconsiderate, rude."

"Sometimes we can't help acting on instinct." She reached out and touched his arm.

"I don't want to do anything to chase you off."

She smiled slyly. "I'm not going anywhere."

He swallowed. "I'm not usually that aggressive."

"No?"

"There's something about you that stirs me," he tried to explain.

Sebastian's words were a trigger, tripping something inside Julie. Passion filled this man. It radiated off him like summer heat. Her heart did a free fall.

"I've spent the last twenty-four hours wondering what you tasted like," he said. "I just had to find out."

"Did I live up to your expectations?"

"You blew them out of the water," he said and kissed her again.

Ditto, she thought, and closed her eyes.

Julie inhaled him, unwrapping his taste layer by layer. There was cinnamon, hot and spicy. He tasted sharp and clean and adventuresome. He knew exactly what he was doing to her. His tongue teased, sending tingles ricocheting around in her mouth, transporting her to an exotic fantasy realm. He kissed with the power and authority born of long practice and she grew jealous of all the other women who'd gotten to kiss him before her. And, she was jealous of all the things she'd missed out on simply because she'd been too afraid to take a chance.

"Excuse me, would you like to order now?" the waitress interrupted.

Grinning, Sebastian's lips slowly left hers. He ordered without even looking at the menu.

Julie's heart skipped a beat. His eyes were dark and commanding and serious and she allowed herself to get lost in them. She had the urge to reach out and brush a finger across the tips of his dark lashes.

"Wow," she said. "That was some kiss."

"Some kiss," he echoed.

They sat staring at each other, neither moving nor saying a thing, simply watching and assessing until a few minutes later the waitress brought their food.

Sebastian took his chopsticks and adroitly picked up a small sushi roll and extended it across the table toward her. "Open your mouth."

"Does it taste fishy?"

"You've never eaten sushi before?"

"No."

He angled his head closer. "Why didn't you tell me? We could have gone somewhere else."

Julie pushed her tongue against the inside of her cheek. "I didn't want to seem unsophisticated. You're so suave and debonair, Mr. Beverly Hills."

He chuckled. "If you only knew."

She leaned forward. "Knew what?"

"Where I came from."

"Oh?"

He shook his head. "That's a story for another time."

Feeling disappointed that he wasn't going to confide in her, Julie sat back in her chair.

"Good thing I ordered a sampler platter. We have a variety to choose from. Since you're a sushi virgin, close your eyes."

"Huh?"

"Close your eyes."

"What for?"

"Epicurean delight."

She felt giggly and the odd feeling unsettled her. The things he could do to her with a simple look was beyond shocking. A strange thrill-chill chased down her spine. Slowly she lowered her lashes, and tentatively put out her tongue.

The second her eyes were closed, she was wishing she hadn't decided to play his game. At least with her eyes open she could see what was coming at her. She tilted her chin up and opened her eyes a slit.

"Nuh-uh, no peeking."

The sushi roll was cool on her tongue and surprisingly delicious. Ginger was the dominant flavor, interlaced with sesame and the earthiness of oyster sauce.

"Mmm," she said, opening her eyes after she'd swallowed. "What's that?"

"It's called Sweet as Sex roll."

She laughed. "You made that up."

"I never joke when it comes to food or sex." He poked a second tidbit with the red-and-black lacquered chopsticks, held it out to her with his palm cupped underneath to catch any drips. "Have another."

His fingertips grazed her chin as she leaned forward to take the bite from his chopsticks. His eyes lit up as he watched her eat. His enjoyment of her pleasure made her knees go weak.

She dabbed her mouth with her napkin. "Exactly what are we doing here, Mr. Black?"

"Call me Sebastian, and we're having lunch."

"You said you invited me out to talk about Confidential Rejuvenations, but I'm getting the feeling you had ulterior motives. Is this a date?"

"Do you want it to be a date?"

Did she? "No."

"Then it's not a date."

"We're strictly here to discuss how I can help you polish Confidential Rejuvenations' image."

Briefly, Sebastian reached up to touch his lips. "After a kiss like that? Sweetheart, you gotta know there's more than just business on my mind."

His honesty clipped her low in the gut. Julie didn't know how to respond. She picked up her own chopsticks and reached for another morsel of sushi to camouflage her indecision.

"Let's keep the conversation on the hospital for now," she said, even though that wasn't what she wanted to talk about. She was too scared to say what she really wanted to discuss.

"All right." He sipped his tea. "So what is your opinion of what's been happening at Confidential Rejuvenations?"

"Personally, I think it's not going to do any good spending money on cleaning up the hospital's reputation as long as there's still someone on the loose wanting to cause damage."

"Dr. Butler and Dr. Covey and Senator Garcia seem to think the person has stopped."

"I think he or she's laying low in the aftermath of the latest scandal over Senator Garcia's daughter trying to kill Tanner."

"What makes you say that?"

Julie shrugged. "A hunch."

"Do you have any ideas on why someone is trying to destroy the hospital's reputation?"

"I suppose it could be a disgruntled ex-employee. Someone who thought they were unfairly dismissed. Or a patient who felt they didn't receive the kind of care they believed they deserved."

Sebastian nodded. "Interesting possibilities."

"Do you have a theory?"

"Me?" He shrugged. "I just got here. I'm simply taking in the lay of the land. That's the reason I'm interviewing Confidential Rejuvenations' employees."

Was it her imagination? Or was there something suggestive about the way he said *lay.* Julie peered at him over the rim of her cup of green tea. "How long are you in town?"

"Until Confidential Rejuvenations' image is cleaned up."

"How long will that take? A week? Two?"

"Maybe a month. Lots of damage control needed on this one."

A month. That was absolutely perfect. Long enough to have a nice, sexual fling, but not so long that she'd fall for him. But how to go about propositioning him? Julie licked her lips.

"You look pensive," he said. "Is there something on your mind?"

"I was thinking about that kiss…."

"So was I." A smile curled his lips.

Julie was nervous about bringing it up, but she wanted him. Not simply because she was looking to spread her sexual wings and not just because she wanted to vanquish Roger.

What she felt was much stronger than either of those motivations. She wanted to feel his hand on her naked thigh. Experience his fingers gently exploring her sex. She longed to know what it would feel like to have his body inside of hers. Looking at him, she was even more convinced he was the antidote she needed.

"I want something else from you," she dared.

That snagged his attention. Sebastian sat up straighter. It was as if he'd just been waiting for her to ask. "What do you need?"

Gulping, Julie forced out the words. "I've heard…um… that you're something of…"

"Yes?"

She wriggled in her chair. "An expert lover."

"Where'd you hear that?"

"Your reputation precedes you."

"Ah." One eyebrow arched up on his forehead.

"Is it true?"

"I don't like to brag."

"Is it true?"

His grin widened. "You tell me. I make love like I kiss."

Whew! If that was true she was in for a lot of fun.

"I've also heard you play the field. That you're not a one-woman man."

"I am a confirmed bachelor."

"Good."

"Good?"

"I'm not looking for anything more than a good time."

"No?" He looked like he didn't believe her.

"No."

"Let me get this straight. Are you propositioning me?"

Don't blush. You can see this through. "I am."

"Hmm." Sebastian seemed both amused and surprised.

"There's one catch, though."

"What's that?"

Bravely, she tilted her chin and asked for what she needed. "Sex is *all* that I want from you."

"Excuse me?"

"I'm attracted to you, you're attracted to me. Neither one of us wants a commitment. Think about it as mutual pleasure-giving. I please you, you please me. We have fun. You go home with fond memories of Austin. I stay here with fond memories of you. It's a win-win situation."

"You wanna be fuck buddies?"

"I wouldn't word it quite that way, but yes."

Suspicion darkened his eyes. "Is this some kind of test? Did Blanche put you up to this? Or was it Linc?"

"Who's Blanche? Who's Linc?"

"Never mind. You're really serious?"

"You have no idea how much courage it took for me to lay my cards on the table. I've never propositioned a man before."

"I applaud your courage."

"So you're in?"

Sebastian held her gaze for a measured moment and then he said, "No."

She blinked. "No?"

It had never occurred to Julie that he would turn her down. They had chemistry. He couldn't deny that. You could start a forest fire with the sparks shooting between them. And he had a reputation as a footloose ladies' man. So why was he turning her down for a torrid meaningless affair?

Face it. You're not pretty enough for him. I mean come on, take a look at the man. He's sexier than any male A-list celebrity.

"No," he reiterated.

"Why not?" she asked and the minute the question was out of her mouth she was wishing she could suck it back in. She did not want to hear him say what she already suspected. He probably dated movie starlets for heaven's sakes. What had she been thinking?

He folded his napkin, laid it on the table beside his plate and signaled the waitress for their check. "Because you're a good girl trying too hard to go bad."

He'd pegged her dead-on. He was too perceptive. "What makes you say that?"

"For one thing, you blush too much."

"Bad girls blush."

"Not so much. And it's more than just the blushing. It's also in the way you eat sushi."

"How's that?"

"Tentative, but eager. And it's in those baby-blue eyes of yours that grow wide when you're shocked or embarrassed. Right now, they're big as plums."

She narrowed her eyes. "You exaggerate."

"Not by much."

"Okay, so what if I am a good girl looking to be bad? What's wrong with that?"

"You can't change who you are. You can try. You can do foolish things, but you can't change your essence. You can't alter your core. And you, Julie DeMarco, are a good girl."

"So what's the deal? Do you only have sex with wicked women?"

"I don't have sex with women who have the potential of falling in love with me. It's a policy of mine."

That made her mad. She pushed back her chair. "You certainly think a lot of your own charm, Mr. Black."

"Hey, I'm trying to protect you. Face facts, you're Cinderella searching for your happily-ever-after ending and I'm no Prince Charming."

Julie got to her feet. "You are the most egotistical man I've ever met. What on earth makes you think I'd fall in love with someone like you?"

"You're a romantic."

"You don't even know me."

"You wear pink scrubs with red hearts on them."

"And you wear designer suits and Gucci shoes and rent expensive sports cars when you're out of town. What are you overcompensating for?" She dropped a purposeful glance at his lap, insinuating he was not well-endowed. It was a low blow. She knew it, but she didn't care.

"If you're trying to crush my ego," he said, getting to his feet, "it won't work. I'm confident in my masculinity."

She snorted and gathered up her purse. This lunch had not turned out the way she'd expected.

"Julie," he said.

She didn't want to answer him, but politeness forced her to turn back toward him. "Yes?"

"It's okay to be yourself. Don't let other people's opinions define who you are," he said.

"I'm not," she denied, but that was exactly what she was doing.

"DO YOU THINK I let other people's opinions define who I am?" Julie asked Vanessa as they struck a cobra pose on side-by-side yoga mats in the exercise room at Confidential Rejuvenations' health club. Two days had passed since her humiliating luncheon with Sebastian and she couldn't stop thinking about him or what he'd said.

You're a good girl trying too hard to go bad.

Well, what was so wrong with trying hard to change things? She was a big believer that if your life wasn't working, it was up to you to fix it. That's what she'd been attempting to do when she'd propositioned him.

"Does this question have anything to do with Sebastian Black?" Vanessa asked, tipping her body in perfect alignment as the instructor told them to push up into downward-facing dog.

"Why would you ask that?"

"You've been moody ever since your lunch date with him and that's not like you at all," Vanessa said on an exhale of air. "What on earth did the man say to get you so agitated?"

"I'm not agitated," Julie denied, struggling to keep up as the instructor had them move into warrior pose.

"Come on, what'd he say?"

Julie inhaled sharply, out of rhythm with the rest of the class. "He said I let other people define who I am."

"This is in response to..."

"I propositioned him."

"You did what!" Cool, smooth Vanessa lost her balance and tumbled over.

"Is there a problem in the back of the class?" asked the instructor.

Vanessa waved a hand. "We're okay."

"I asked him if he was interested in a fling with me and he said no."

"Ooh, serious ego blow. Did he say why not?"

"Yeah, he gave me that line about not letting other people define who I am and he said I was a good girl trying too hard to go bad."

"He's got a point." Vanessa stretched.

"He said he didn't want me falling in love with him. As if!"

Vanessa clicked her tongue. They were both out of step with the rest of the class now. "He's got you pegged."

Julie gave up all pretense at trying to do yoga and sank her hands on her hips. "You don't think I'm capable of having a no-strings-attached affair?"

"Come on, you're the queen of romance. You kept all the homecoming mums from high school, you have a hope chest and a hundred stuffed animals on your bed."

"That is a clear exaggeration. I only have four stuffed animals."

"That's four too many for anyone over the age of sixteen."

"They have sentimental value."

"Hence my accusation that you're the queen of romance."

"You're right." Julie smacked her forehead with a palm. "I am a hopeless romantic, and I'm trying to rectify it, but Sebastian Black won't cooperate."

"Actually," Vanessa said, "I think it's kind of sweet that he doesn't want to hurt you. Most guys would just take you up on your offer and not care if you got your heart trampled."

Julie rolled her eyes. "He's assuming a lot about me."

"You gotta admit, he's pretty dead-on."

"Am I that easy to read?"

"Yep. Remember there are other guys in the world."

"Maybe so, but Sebastian's the one who turns me on."

The yoga instructor cleared her throat. "Are you sure there's not a problem back there?"

Julie rolled up her mat.

"Hey, where are you going? We've another fifteen minutes left in class."

"You soldier on."

"Hang on, I'll come with." Vanessa rolled up her mat and trotted after her. "Jules, come on, don't get your feelings hurt."

"My feelings aren't hurt," she denied as they walked out of the class together. "I'm just feeling…"

"What?"

Julie sighed. "Like I'm missing out. I'm tired of being a good girl. I want to have fun. I want to be wild and reckless and naughty."

"No one's stopping you."

Julie met Vanessa's eyes. "Okay, so what should I do about Sebastian? How do I get him to crack?"

Vanessa grinned. "He's a guy. It shouldn't be that hard. Just seduce him."

"Um…how?"

"What do you mean *how?*"

"I've never seduced a guy before."

"Seriously?"

Julie shrugged. "What can I say? I never felt the need to seduce anyone before now. Roger and Phillip both pursued me with the full-court press."

"I can't believe you've never seduced a guy. Have you ever done a striptease?"

"No. Will you help teach me what I need to know?"

"Chica," said Vanessa, who used to be an exotic dancer before she went to medical school. "You've come to the right place."

HIS CAMPAIGN was no good.

Morosely, Sebastian sat propped up in bed, staring at the PR plan on his computer screen that he'd created for Confidential Rejuvenations. It stunk like month-old garbage and the hell of it was he had no idea how to fix it. He'd already rejected over two dozen ideas.

It was Thursday evening and he was holed up in his hotel room. It had been two days since his ill-fated lunch with Julie. Two eternal days in which he could not get her out of his mind long enough to effectively do his job. No woman had ever derailed his concentration like this and he was mystified.

Repeatedly, he kept replaying what had happened in the sushi restaurant. How he'd kissed her without even considering the consequences. How his body had hardened and his heart had galloped and he'd felt…*overcome.*

Then he thought about how she'd asked him to become

her lover and he'd turned her down. What was the matter with him? He'd never turned down a willing, single woman in his life.

He'd wanted to accept her offer. He'd ached to scoop her up in his arms and carry her off to some place and have his way with her. But if he were being completely honest with himself, he'd have to admit, she scared the living hell out of him.

The arc of sexual electricity between them was so strong, it could power a medium-sized city for a year. He'd never experienced anything like it and he couldn't decide what it meant. He'd just known he couldn't make love to her.

Not when he was feeling so susceptible.

Coward.

Hey, better to be a coward than to end up…*what?* What was he afraid was going to happen if he had sex with her?

He'd never been so inarticulate in his life, but when it came to the sensations Julie stirred in him there were simply no words.

Chuffing in a deep breath, he ran a hand through his hair and stared at his computer screen. Why couldn't he concentrate? Why did all his ideas feel flat? How come every time he tried to visualize a blockbuster spin campaign, he saw Julie's arresting features instead?

Face it, she's got you so horny you can't think straight.

Dammit. He had to stop this. But how?

Make love to her. That'll get her out of your system.

But were the potential complications worth the risk? She could deny it all she wanted, but Julie DeMarco was the happily-ever-after type. The sort you brought home to Mama for Thanksgiving dinner. For some reason she was trying too hard to act wild. Her motivation was what concerned him most. Why had she propositioned him out of the blue? Was she trying to get back at a boyfriend?

So what if she was? Revenge sex could be pretty damned hot.

Sebastian looked at the crumpled papers all around him, thought of the PR campaign that was going nowhere and realized he didn't have much of a choice.

Just then, there was a knock on the door. Grateful for the distraction, he put his laptop aside, got up and went to answer it. He found a bellboy standing in the hallway. "Yes?"

"Package for Mr. Black."

He took the big box, gave the guy a generous tip and lugged it into the room. His name and room number were written on the box, but that was it. No return address.

Curiosity had him cutting the ribbon and ripping off the brown paper wrapping. He took off the lid and peered inside. He laughed at the pair of black cowboy boots, matching black Stetson and a brand-new lasso.

At the bottom of the box was a folded note.

> I'm naughtier than you could ever guess, cowboy. Wear this outfit and meet me at Lone Star riding stables adjacent to Confidential Rejuvenations on Sunday at 10:00 a.m. That is if you have the balls.

Instant sweat popped out on his forehead as heat licked through his belly. Sebastian flipped the note over searching for a signature, but instead of a name he found the following postscript.

> PS—Expect the unexpected.

5

Expect the unexpected.

Julie's rousing postscript ricocheted through Sebastian's mind. Did she have any idea how seductive those words were? His interest was provoked, his curiosity piqued, his desire for sexual adventure fueled. His entire body tingled with heightened awareness.

He thought about the kiss they'd shared in the restaurant. The memory escalated his anticipation. He had three condoms tucked into his shirt pocket. He couldn't recall the last time he'd been this crazed with lust.

This woman was a lot more complicated than first impressions led him to believe.

It was just before ten o'clock on Sunday morning and Sebastian paced the visitors' parking lot of the Lone Star riding stables. He had learned from his research on Confidential Rejuvenations that the hospital had a contract with the riding stables to provide therapeutic recreation for inpatients undergoing treatment, and Confidential Rejuvenations' employees were allowed to ride for free. In exchange, the stable owners got discounted health care.

He wore the outfit Julie had sent. Black cowboy boots, Stetson, lasso slung over his shoulder. Plus, he'd added jeans and a Western shirt he'd bought at his hotel's gift shop. He felt like a big dork, but no one had paid the slightest bit of attention to him, so maybe he blended in better than he thought.

In the green pastures of the expansive paddock, well-cared-for horses grazed. The animals made him think of his childhood and thinking of his childhood made him antsy. He'd traded fields for asphalt for a reason.

Five minutes passed.

He paced the parking lot. Where was she? A flick of his wrist and he checked his watch. She'd said ten. He was sure of it. He pulled the note out of his wallet to double-check. Yep, 10:00 a.m. It was now eight minutes past the hour.

Another couple of minutes passed and he fretted that she'd stood him up.

Had she stood him up?

The knot in his stomach tightened. Sebastian had never been stood up in his life. Was she intentionally making him wait? Heightening the anticipation?

If that was the case, she'd hit the nail on the head. His self-control shredded.

Or had she simply chickened out?

As Sebastian was about to reach for his cell phone and give her a call, she pulled in to the parking lot in her fuel-efficient hybrid car—that Linc's fiancée would approve of—and got out.

One look at her and Sebastian lost his breath.

She was dressed in fawn-colored jodhpurs and black paddock boots, and she carried a riding crop. The sight of her looking all Lady Chatterley caused the muscles along his shoulders to twitch.

As if in a trance, famished for sex, the raw scent of stable combined with her feminine essence threw him back to his youth. To his first sexual experience. He'd lost his virginity on the commune. To one of Aunt Bunnie's hippie friends. He'd been sixteen, the woman a good twenty years older. He'd gone into the barn that day a boy and walked out a man.

Sebastian's attention locked on her. Adrenaline fused with testosterone. The combination charged through his veins like an infection, blasting him with a feverish heat.

She strutted right past him.

Ignoring him.

For a second he felt slighted and then he realized it was all part of her seduction.

Expect the unexpected.

Mesmerized, he turned and followed her.

She opened the gate and walked up to the stable entrance, where an older woman in faded blue jeans was tying a quarter horse to a circular walker.

"You wanna ride?" the woman asked, eyeing her attire.

"May I look at the horses first?" Julie asked. "I work at Confidential Rejuvenations and I was told I could select my own mount."

"Sure." The woman shrugged. "Have a look around."

"Thanks," Julie said.

Then the woman caught sight of Sebastian. He watched her eyes light up as she raked a glance over him and said in a husky voice, "How 'bout you, cowboy? You ready to ride?"

Sebastian jerked a thumb at Julie. "I'm with her."

The woman looked sorely disappointed. "I'll be up at the bunkhouse. Just give me a holler when you folks pick out your steeds and I'll saddle 'em up for you."

"Thank you." Julie nodded and sashayed into the large, clean stables.

Watching her ass sway in those jodhpurs hardened his

cock. Surely she didn't intend for them to have a tryst right here in the stables in broad daylight.

Did she?

The barn smelled of fresh paint, horses and hay. They passed the tack room containing saddles, bridles, ropes and other riding equipment. Ahead of him, Julie was flicking the riding crop as if she knew precisely how to use it. His skin stung just thinking about it and, although he wouldn't have believed it possible, he got even harder.

From the stalls came the sound of horses chomping their feed. Julie peeped in one stall after another, murmuring to the animals. She still hadn't spoken a word to him and her mysterious air was shooting his lust to a whole new level. After they'd past the first set of stalls, Sebastian trailing behind her, Julie stopped and pulled a pair of gloves from her hip pocket. Slowly, she worked her fingers into the expensive, supple leather.

Sebastian bit down on his bottom lip to keep from groaning.

She paused at the next stall. "Well, hello there, handsome," she cooed. "Would you like a sweet treat?"

The horse nickered.

Julie drew a sugar cube from her breast pocket and held it out to him. With surprising gentleness, the stallion took the sugar cube from her palm.

Sebastian moved closer.

Julie turned her back to him and headed up a stairway leading to the hayloft. The riding boots she wore made provocative scraping noises against the wood.

He threw a glance over his shoulder. The woman in the faded jeans was no longer in sight. Except for the horses, the stables were empty, but he knew anyone could walk in at any time. The thought had his balls drawing up tight against him.

Julie disappeared into the next level of the barn.

Sebastian made a beeline after her. His heart suddenly thumped so loudly he feared the noise of it would echo throughout the stables and alert the staff to the sexual shenanigans afoot.

Once he was inside the hayloft, Sebastian had to pause and let his eyes adjust to the dimness. The only light came from the stairway they'd just tracked up and one small, narrow window at the top of the loft.

He blinked. Where was Julie?

After a couple of seconds, he spotted her. At the very back of the loft, lounging on a pile of hay, her fingers slowly undoing the buttons of her shirt, a wicked smile on her sweet face.

Excitement twisting his gut, Sebastian said, "Julie, you're so freakin' hot."

Her smile widened and she lowered her eyelashes. "My name isn't Julie. You may call me Lady Chatterley, stable boy."

All the blood left his brain, rushed headlong into his groin. He went to her and dropped to one knee. "Your wish is my command, mistress."

She undid the last button, allowing her blouse to fall open to reveal a lacy pink bra, then she picked up her riding crop and slapped it softly against her gloved palm.

"Take off your pants," she commanded. "And lie down."

His hand trembled with excitement. Her feminine scent teased his nostrils. Her challenge provoked him. His muscles tensed. Her seduction was almost more than he could stand.

Their gazes struck, sparked.

Sweat rolled down his neck.

Julie's pupils widened. She flicked out her tongue to moisten her lips.

Was it his imagination or was she breathing as heavily as he?

It didn't matter where they were, or that they could be interrupted at any time. They could have been on the moon. They could have been in the middle of rush-hour traffic. He was aware of nothing except her.

As reckless as it might be, he had to have her or go mad.

Suddenly, he realized how little he knew about her, but it really didn't matter. In fact, the mystery of her only escalated his need.

He'd never felt a thrill quite like this. Not when he was grandstanding in front of the media. Not when he was boldly salvaging a client's reputation. Not when he was speeding on the Pacific Coast Highway in his Ferrari.

This was an adventure.

The blood pumping hotly through his veins shoved him into action. He shucked his boots and pants and looked over at her.

She cracked the whip.

Goose bumps fled up his arms. On the level below them they could hear horses moving around in their stalls, bumping against their enclosures.

His mind spun. What would she do next? Her audaciousness stirred him. What else did she have in her bag of tricks?

The taste of his escalating desire spilled into his mouth, raw and peppery. He couldn't stop looking at her. Her blue eyes shone with desire. Her long blond hair swung loose as she propped herself up on one elbow so she could look up at him.

The wanton expression in her eyes slammed his libido

into fifth gear. He dropped onto the floor beside her. Slowly she licked her lips, and then moved to straddle him.

Hormones, blazing and powerful, shot to his groin. The circuitry of his brain fired, sending hungry electrical impulses to his nerves, his muscles, his every cell.

Ah, Lady Chatterley tasted of peppermint and red-hot passion. She slipped her tongue between his teeth.

He opened his mouth.

Their tongues waltzed. First she was the instigator, stealing his breath, numbing his mind, but then he took over.

He reached up to slide his hands up her waist to her breasts, pushing his fingers underneath her bra to lightly pinch her nipples until they beaded hard as pebbles.

Lady Chatterley hissed in her breath. "Yesss."

He grinned, happy to have elicited such a response. He raised his head to draw one of those hot little nipples into his mouth. She tasted like heaven.

Gently, he flipped her over onto her back. He peeled off her boots and by the time he was done, she'd already plucked off the gloves and was unzipping her fly, fumbling at the buckle of her brown leather belt. He grabbed her at the waist and she lifted her hips as he pulled off the jodhpurs along with her pink thong panties.

When her pants were off, she lay back against the hay, clothed only in the pink lace bra. He splayed a palm across the tautness of her flat belly, just above the beautiful golden triangle of hair at her pubis.

He gazed into her eyes, looking, really looking at her. What delicate skin. What fine bone structure. Up next to her refined features, her petite body, he felt like some giant peasant. She was cut from the most expensive cloth, he from a burlap bag, and he worried that he might hurt her.

"It's not fair."

"What's not?" he asked, mesmerized.

"I'm naked and you're not. I want to see your body, Sebastian."

He wrestled out of his shirt and whipped off his Stetson.

But he kept his underwear on, just to tease.

Her eyes were beaded on his erection straining against his boxer briefs.

"Come here." She patted a spot to her left.

He obeyed, settled into the hay beside her.

Sebastian was damned good at foreplay. He liked to play. He enjoyed taking his time. But suddenly he was at a loss. With her, he didn't know where to begin.

"Listen, Julie…" His voice came out so tight and brittle he scarcely recognized it.

"Just kiss me, Sebastian. There's no need to overthink this."

He closed his lips over hers. The kiss was heated, but tentative, exploring. She opened her mouth wider and then slowly spread her legs.

Sebastian ran his hand lower. After a few minutes, as their kissing grew more urgent and he slowly stroked her golden hair, his fingers moved downward in lazy circles until he reached the warm, moist folds of her sex. She was damp with desire, but he wanted her soaking wet and begging for release.

"Mmm," she murmured and shifted against his hand. "That feels good."

He slipped his index finger into her.

She sucked in a gasp of air and her eyes widened with pleasure. He liked seeing what he was doing to her.

"I want to touch you, too," she said. "Take off your underwear."

He obeyed her and tossed his briefs away, then nestled beside her once more.

"I guess I was wrong." She eyed him in the dim light.

"Wrong about what?"

"When I accused you of overcompensating for something."

He had enough of an ego that her comment made him smile.

With one smooth palm, she reached down to cup his balls in her hand. Her touch felt dangerously good. Sebastian thought he was going to lose it right there. He bit down on his lip to hold back the groan rising in his throat. He closed his eyes, fighting the urge to come.

Gently, she tickled him. Her caress injected a whole new facet of awareness into their game. His mind spun. What was she up to?

"Hey," he said, "you better back off that for now."

Truth was, he had to concentrate on not coming. He tightened his stomach muscles and went back to kissing her, stroking her. His fingers strummed her soft skin.

He thought of all the romantic things he would normally say to a woman he was having sex with, but now everything he could think of sounded trite. Where had his glibness gone? Where were the sweet nothings that usually fell so easily from his tongue? He wished he knew what to say, but he just didn't. All his usual lines and flattery failed him so he just said the truth. "I'm glad to be here with you."

"Me, too." Her smile warmed him like sunshine and melted the lump blocking his throat.

His cock throbbed, wanting to be inside her. But in that moment, Sebastian realized something. This was all about her. He was going to give her the pleasure she sought and he was taking himself out of the equation. He was going to meet her needs first and worry about his own second.

He unhooked her bra, dipped his head and took one perky pink nipple into his mouth and sucked lightly, while his hand strayed back to that heavenly triangle between her firm thighs. He slipped a finger inside her again and she was wetter than before.

"Sebastian." She breathed his name on a sigh and ran her fingers through his hair, down his face.

Her touch was a feather, but he felt it all the way to the tip of his erect shaft. Blood drained from his head, ran down to satisfy his cock. It took every ounce of strength of will he possessed not to jam himself inside her.

He spent more time at her nipples, teasing and licking, sucking and nipping until she was moaning as softly as a humming top. Once her chest was heaving and her fingers were knotted in his hair, he slowly moved from her breasts to her sternum, planting hot kisses down, down, down to her navel.

The lower he went the faster and shallower her breathing grew. Muscles all along her body tightening in response.

"Wait," she gasped, when his mouth was almost at the gateway at the most feminine part of her.

"What is it?" he whispered.

"No one's ever…"

He raised his head. "Yes?"

"No one has ever loved me like that."

"No one's ever gone down on you?"

She shook her head. "I've never had much luck with oral sex."

"Well, sweetheart," he said, a flicker of his smooth-talking self showing up, "your luck has just changed."

Okay, so he was bragging, but he wanted to heighten her anticipation.

But what if you can't make good on your promise?

He would. Or die trying.

She made a happy noise and for a moment, he had to rock back on his heels and look at her naked body from the top of her blond head to the rosy pink folds of her womanhood.

The expression in her blue eyes was languid, sultry. She watched him watching her. She was ready.

The barn had gone completely silent. In the stables below the horses had stopped moving. It was as if no world existed between this circle of two.

Sebastian settled between her legs and lowered his head. Softly, he blew his warm breath against her tender membranes and gently edged her knees farther apart with his shoulders. He couldn't wait to taste her.

He pressed his mouth to her sweet lips, heard her sharp intake of breath, felt her inner thigh muscles quiver.

She tasted even better than he'd imagined. Fresh and tangy and womanly. He loved the intimacy of exploring her most precious place with his lips. Her every thought was translated in her movements and he read her with his tongue. A slight shift in her hips and he corrected, moving right and left, up and down until he had her purring like an expensive engine.

He loved what his mouth was doing to her, whisking her away on a sea of sensation. She was so responsive to everything he did.

Reverently, he suckled her veiled hood. He ached to be inside her. To feel her pulse around him. He wanted to join her, to fly to the stars with her, but he would not. This was all about her. He hadn't earned his reputation as a good lover by being selfish.

Sensing that she was edging toward ecstasy, Sebastian adroitly strummed his tongue against her straining clit.

The orgasm teased her, elusive but near. He could feel it inside her. Pressing…pressing…pressing. Closer and closer. Lifting, soaring, ready to converge.

"That's it, sweetheart," he cooed. "Let yourself go."

She responded with a fervency that shook him. He'd never watched a woman react like this. She rode his attention. Rode it hard and fast and full as he made love to her with his mouth.

Then it happened. Julie let out a strangled cry, tensed in his arms. He felt her muscles contract against his tongue. Her body glistened with perspiration.

He moved up, wrapped his arms around her and they lay there in the hay sweating, shuddering, panting for breath.

He had an unexpected hankering to linger there. To cradle her in his arms, kiss her face, brush her hair from her eyes, tell her how absolutely wonderful she was. He didn't get these kinds of urges, dammit, and he wasn't sure he liked them, so it was something of a relief when she pulled back before he could act on the impulses.

She was up, moving away from him, bending down to retrieve her clothes. Giving him a spectacular view of her ass.

She was dressing, zipping up her pants, raking her fingers through her hair to dislodge bits of hay, buttoning up her shirt. She tossed his pants to him and he grabbed them with a one-handed catch.

"Hey," he said, shimmying into his pants. "Why don't we go get some brunch?"

"No, Sebastian—"

"What? You don't eat brunch? Come on, you can't tell me eggs Benedict wouldn't be good right now."

"Listen, I've got some ground rules for our affair."

"Ground rules? Affair?"

"Yes, I want to have fun, but I don't want either of us to get hurt."

Damn if she didn't sound exactly like him when approaching a woman about a new sexual relationship. It felt odd being on the receiving end of such a declaration. He cupped his hands around both ears. "I'm all ears."

She wrapped a hand around her waist. "Please don't make me laugh."

"Why not? Sex isn't serious business."

"I know, but I want to make sure you hear me."

He pulled her to him and kissed her on the forehead, then on her eyelids and the tip of her nose. "So about these ground rules. Whatcha got?"

She pushed away from him. "No dating. No going out to eat or to the movies or long walks in the moonlight. This is only about hot sex."

"I can do that."

"And don't tell me anything personal about your life and I won't tell you anything personal about mine."

"Fair enough."

"And this is not romance. When it's over, when you go back to your life in California, it's over. Got it?"

"Are you really sure this is what you want?"

"Yes," she said, slipping into her riding boots. "And don't look so crestfallen. I'm sure you're accustomed to brief, satisfying sexual encounters."

He was, but not today. Not now and certainly not with her. The realization that he wanted to spend the rest of the day with her was disturbing. Especially when it seemed that the last thing she wanted was to spend any more time with him.

"See ya." She wriggled her fingers at him and disappeared down the steps.

"Hey," he called, "wait for me."

She didn't wait and by the time he'd found his boots and made it down the steps and out of the stables, Julie was already getting into her car.

Leaving Sebastian feeling lonelier than he'd ever felt in his life.

HIDDEN IN THE COPSE of trees on the property separating Confidential Rejuvenations from the Lone Star riding stables, unseen by either Sebastian or Julie, a shadowy figure lurked.

So Julie DeMarco and Sebastian Black had brought their little game of slap and tickle closer to home. Just who in the hell did they think they were? Flaunting their affair like a couple of horny teenagers.

Disgusting.

Well, a kink was about to be thrown into their cute sex party.

They had to be punished. Made to pay for their sins.

And a great big sex scandal starring the spin doctor and the slutty home-wrecking nurse should do the trick quite nicely.

JAZZED UP, Julie went to Confidential Rejuvenations the following Monday morning humming under her breath and smiling at everyone she met. She'd come in two hours early to take a prep test before trying again for her certifying exam to become a sex counselor.

Devi Parker, a certified sex therapist and Julie's mentor, proctored the test in her office. Devi was an attractive, dark-haired forty-year-old woman who'd been married ten years to an Austin cop, and had two great kids. She successfully juggled her career and family and made it look easy. Julie aspired to be like her someday.

"You're chipper this morning," Devi said, slipping the test booklet on the desk in front of Julie. "Did you have a nice weekend?"

"I did," she answered.

"Good for you. It's great to see you looking so happy." Devi set the egg timer on her desk. "You have forty-five minutes to complete part one, then you can take a break and come back to tackle part two."

Julie dove right into the task, her mind supercharged. She didn't hesitate or stumble over the questions like she had when she'd taken the qualifying exam last month. She breezed through the first section in thirty minutes.

"You have time. You can go back and double-check your work," Devi told her.

"It's okay. I'm ready to go on to the next half. I don't need a break."

Devi tilted her head and gave Julie a curious look. "That must have been some weekend."

"It was." She grinned.

"I have a feeling a guy was involved."

Julie smiled wider.

"That explains it." Devi smiled back. "Are you sure you don't need a break?"

"I'm good to go, bring on the test."

Somehow, even though she couldn't explain it, what had happened in that hayloft inspired her. It was as if the universe had aligned and everything was going her way. Why in the heck had she waited so long to have playful, no-strings-attached sex? She felt giddy and free and so alive.

More alive than she'd ever felt in her life. Neither Roger nor Phillip had ever made her feel like this.

And she couldn't get enough of it. The sensation was seriously addicting. She wanted more casual sex and lots of it.

She finished her test and handed it to Devi.

"Go get a cup of coffee and when you come back I'll have it graded for you," her mentor said.

"Thanks." Julie picked up her purse and wandered down to the coffee kiosk on the first floor. After grabbing a light mocha latte, she turned to head back upstairs, but caught sight of Sebastian standing in the corridor with a group of people. It looked as if they were waiting for someone to come unlock the door to a meeting room. He was busy chatting and he hadn't seen her.

Pulse racing, Julie dodged behind a large potted ficus so that she could watch him unobserved.

He migrated from person to person, shaking hands, clasping shoulders, charming the congregation with his winning smile. Today, he wore a black turtleneck, form-fitting black trousers that showed off his breathtaking physique and a houndstooth sports jacket. Because of the turtleneck, he wasn't wearing one of his colorful power ties and she found she missed his personality-defining accessory. His jet-black hair was, as always, neatly combed.

Julie's attraction to him zoomed beyond her control. He was the most incredible man in the hospital and she was sleeping with him.

His profile was dazzling. Regal nose, strong chin, chiseled cheekbones. He was witty and charming and gracious and irresistible. Several women in his group were openly staring at him.

Wistfulness swept through Julie and she found herself wishing there could be more between them besides sex.

Don't be stupid. He'd just break your heart. You're in this for a good time and nothing more. So have a good time and let that be enough.

Her cell phone vibrated. She switched the latte to her left hand, fished the phone from the pocket of her scrub jacket with her right and flipped it open.

"You made a ninety-six!" Devi's excited voice greeted her.

"Really?"

"Whatever you did this weekend, keep doing it. Obviously it's working. I'm so excited for you. You're going to ace that exam this time, Julie. I'll sign you up to retest in November."

"Thanks," she said, as a warm glow stole over her. She shivered with happiness. She was so close to achieving her goal and she had Sebastian to thank for it.

"See you in group," Devi said. "Congrats again."

"'Bye." Julie hung up, slipped the cell phone back into her pocket. Her gaze shot back to Sebastian and she had the strongest urge to tell him about acing her prep test.

But she didn't want the whole hospital to know they were seeing each other. Still, it was tempting and she almost started down the corridor toward him when the side exit door opened and her ex-lover, Roger Marshall, stepped into the building and made a beeline for Sebastian.

6

"HELLO." AN OLDER MAN with salt-and-pepper hair in a gray tweed suit reached out to shake Sebastian's hand. "I'm Roger Marshall, Keeley's father. I'm the one who recommended your firm to Confidential Rejuvenations."

"Thank you." Sebastian smiled. He and Roger stepped into the conference room with the other board members. His guard went up at the mention of Keeley's name, but he was too good of a PR expert to let his personal feelings show.

"Lincoln speaks glowingly of the work you do and since we're about to become family, I thought why not throw business your way?" Roger's smile seemed genuine.

"You're all for this wedding?"

"You're not?"

"They seem so young."

"Lincoln is a wonderful guy. So full of promise and he's a true hero and an honor to our country. I'd be proud to call him son."

Okay then. "But your daughter's not even through college."

Roger shrugged. "You love who you love, right? She's twenty-one. It's better to be supportive than antagonistic. And like I said, I admire and respect your brother. Keeley's lucky to have him."

Yes, she is.

"Are you on the hospital board?" Sebastian asked, changing the subject.

"I resigned from the board a couple of months ago, but one of the other board members is off on medical leave and they asked me to step in. I'm up to speed on what's been happening. We're eager to see your plans for revamping Confidential Rejuvenations' image."

"That's what we're here for. Have a seat, Mr. Marshall."

"Please, call me Roger. We're going to be family, after all."

"Right."

Sebastian had come up with a three-tiered plan of attack for countering the bad publicity the boutique hospital had suffered over the course of the past year. He had a PowerPoint presentation set up that wowed the audience and by the time he finished his pitch, the board enthusiastically approved the strategies he'd outlined.

"My only concern is the same one I've heard expressed by several hospital employees." Sebastian clicked off the PowerPoint presentation. "I can guarantee results with this plan, as long as there are no more…um…unsettling occurrences. Considering all that has happened, one more scandal could be Confidential Rejuvenations' Waterloo."

Several board members nodded.

"Confidential Rejuvenations' third-quarter profits are already down twenty percent following the adverse publicity in the fallout from the attempt on Tanner Doyle's life."

"That's why we hired you," Dr. Butler said.

Sebastian nodded. "Granted, most people seem to think that Chloe Garcia's stabbing of your head of security wasn't connected to the hospital saboteur, but I'm not so convinced. Chloe had a fragile mental history and after discussing the incident with her father, Senator

Garcia, I believe someone manipulated the susceptible woman's behavior."

A murmur of speculation ran through the group.

"Luckily, the saboteur has not made a move in several weeks. The question is, can we safely assume that he or she has obtained what gratifications they were seeking and have ceased to cause problems? Or have they simply been lying in wait, planning their coup de grace? I'm going to let Tanner tell you about the new security measures he's instituting."

Sebastian turned the podium over to Tanner, who discussed what his team had been doing to thwart further sabotage. When he was finished, there was a discussion among the board members. Finally, they came to a consensus.

"We want you to go ahead with your PR work," Dr. Butler said. "It can't hurt to get started."

Sebastian folded his arms over his chest. "And if something else happens?"

"In that case, at least you'll be on hand to step in and smooth things over with the press."

"All right, I'll get started right away," Sebastian agreed, even though he couldn't seem to shake the feeling that somehow all of this would backfire…

JULIE HAD TO FIND OUT what Roger was doing at Confidential Rejuvenations and she had to do it without letting Sebastian know her connection to him.

Because she'd finished her prep test much earlier than she'd expected, she had some time before her shift started. She'd hang around and see if she could catch Sebastian after his meeting. But she had to do it without being seen by Roger. The last thing she wanted was to come face-to-face with her ex. Especially after he'd sent her that note.

She lurked in the lobby until she saw the meeting break up. Sebastian came out of the conference room with Roger. They shook hands, then Roger left the hospital and Sebastian started toward the elevator.

"Sebastian," she called out to him.

He stopped at the elevator and turned toward her. His eyes lit up and a big grin broke across his face. "Julie."

"Hi," she breathed.

"Hi."

They simply stood there looking at each other.

"I had a great time yesterday," he finally said.

"I did, too." She so wanted to tell him about acing her prep test but suddenly remembered her ground rules. They weren't supposed to share personal information with each other.

"Did you need something?" he asked. "I was on my way to another meeting."

"No, no, I just wanted to say hi." She raised a hand. "Hi."

She wished he would ask her out, but he couldn't ask her out because she'd told him not to. Why had she told him not to ask her out? Oh, yeah, so she wouldn't get attached to him.

He raised his hand, mirroring her. "Hi."

The elevator dinged as it settled to the ground floor. He jerked his thumb toward the lift. "I've got another meeting to go to. Is there anything else?"

"No."

"Sure there's nothing I can do for you?" His eyes were teasing.

"Um…I was wondering who that man was you were talking to in the corridor?" she blurted.

Smooth, very smooth, DeMarco.

"You mean Roger Marshall?"

"Is that his name?" Mentally she groaned. She was making a mess of this. "Is he a board member?"

"Used to be, retired, now he's back filling in for someone." People got off the elevator, Sebastian stepped on, he put a hand out to hold the door open. "You going up?"

"Sure, why not?" She hopped on, her nerves stretched tight. She was mucking it up big-time.

"What floor?" he asked.

"Five, please."

He pressed the buttons for both the fourth and fifth floors. The doors closed. They stood side by side, staring at the lighted button panel. Julie had her purse clutched under her arm, using it as a barrier between them.

"He's my future in-law," Sebastian said.

"Who is?"

"Roger."

The impact of what he said hit her like a slap. She felt as if she was going to throw up. "You're engaged to Roger's daughter?"

He laughed. "I thought our agreement was not to get personal."

"If you're engaged," she said, "the agreement, not to mention our affair, is null and void."

"*I'm* not engaged to Roger's daughter," he soothed. "Keeley's marrying my younger brother, Lincoln."

"Oh," she said. That made it better, but not by much. He was still peripherally connected to Roger.

"Roger's the one who recommended my services to Confidential Rejuvenations."

"Oh," she said again, knowing she sounded stupid.

The elevator stopped on the fourth floor.

"When do you want to get together again?" Sebastian asked as the door slid open.

She stared at him, feeling blindsided. *You gotta end this thing, now. You can't have an affair with someone who's about to become family with your married ex-lover.*

Gosh, that sounded so soap opera–like.

It was all too complicated and way more than she bargained for. She had to bail out of this thing before she got in too deep. "I'll call you," she said as the doors slid closed, but she knew in her heart she was never going to make that call.

"YOU'VE BEEN AWFULLY quiet all week, Jules," Elle said. "Anything you want to tell us?"

It was Friday evening and Elle and Dante were throwing a backyard barbecue as a housewarming for the new home they'd recently purchased together.

Julie hadn't talked to Sebastian since their conversation in the elevator. She hadn't called him, nor had he called her. She told herself she was glad, but she was lying.

While the women were sitting at the picnic table munching on crudités, the men gathered around Dante's high-tech barbecue grill he'd purchased for the occasion. The group included Dante, Tanner, Carlisle Jones, who was the head of maintenance at Confidential Rejuvenations, and anesthesiologist Brad Mertz. They were grunting and high-fiving over the butane setup and stainless-steel utensils.

"Are they actually making caveman noises?" Vanessa asked, dredging a baby carrot in ranch dressing dip.

Elle waved a hand. "Boys and their toys. As long as the meat gets grilled, I don't care what they do. So fill us in, Jules. What's happening with you and that hunky spin doctor?"

"Um, it didn't work out."

"What do you mean?"

Julie shrugged. She didn't want to talk about it in front of Carlisle's wife, Bridget, or Brad's date, Sabrina, a new scrub nurse who'd just started working at Confidential Rejuvenations. "His brother is marrying my ex's daughter," she said, hoping her friends would pick up the clue without her having to elaborate in front of Bridget and Sabrina. "Kinda complicates things."

"Ah," Elle said. "Gotcha. We'll talk later."

Julie breathed a sigh of relief as Elle steered the conversation toward safer territory.

"Steaks are done," Dante called out. "Load up your plates everyone."

Grateful for the distraction, Julie grabbed a paper plate and headed for the buffet. The filet mignon did smell delicious.

They were all sitting down at the patio picnic tables, when the redwood gate swung inward.

"Is this where the party is?" asked a masculine voice.

A very familiar masculine voice.

Sebastian.

"Hey, you made it." Dante rose from the table to cross the yard and clap Sebastian on the back. "I thought we were going to have to send out a search party."

"Come on in." Elle got up to join her husband.

"Thanks for inviting me…." Sebastian said, but his words broke off when his eyes met Julie's.

"We're happy to have you. Come on, get a plate," Elle encouraged.

"She invited Sebastian?" Julie hissed between clenched teeth to Vanessa who was sitting beside her.

"She thought you'd like the idea."

"I don't like the idea. Bad idea. Bad Elle. Why didn't she tell me she invited him?"

"You know how Elle likes to play matchmaker ever since she hooked up with Dante. She got Brad and Sabrina together." Vanessa put an arm around her. "It'll be okay."

"I don't need a match made. That's the whole point. To have sex without getting emotionally involved. No matches should be made where I'm concerned."

"Sebastian's coming this way. You can yell at Elle later. In the meantime, smile."

Yes, he was looking delicious in a long-sleeved forest-green polo shirt and a pair of blue jeans that molded to his muscular butt and showed off his long, lean athletic legs. He had a bottle of wine tucked under one arm and the expression of a man who'd been caught by surprise, but was too adroit to show it.

Clearly, he hadn't expected to see her any more than she'd expected to see him.

Sebastian blinked, unable to believe his good fortune. Julie was here. Immediately, his spirits lightened. And to think he'd almost decided not to come by tonight.

He'd planned on spending the weekend alone, working on the campaign. He also wanted to figure out what was happening to him where Julie was concerned, and why it bothered the hell out of him that she hadn't called him like she said she would. But then he'd gotten back to his empty hotel room at the end of the week, and he knew the only way to get her out of his head was to be with other people.

Now here she was. Looking damned gorgeous in a red sweater and blue jeans. He hungered to know what it would feel like to be inside of her. He'd been imagining it all week.

Dammit, he was getting a boner.

To distract himself, he handed the Shiraz he'd brought to Elle, picked up a plate and headed for the buffet table. He loaded up on food, not even paying attention to what he was getting. Julie muddled him that much.

"Scoot down everyone." Elle waved a hand. "Make room for Sebastian."

Dante shifted, creating an opening on his side of the table directly across from Julie.

But Julie wasn't looking at Sebastian, rather she was attacking her baked potato with the gusto of a someone who hadn't eaten in a week. Was she really that hungry? Or was it a dodge so she wouldn't have to look at him?

Several moments passed, and he was certain now she was avoiding him, but he didn't know why. What misstep had he made? Had he not satisfied her in the hayloft? Had she faked her orgasm? His male ego flattened at the notion. She had seemed distant all week. But he hadn't pushed her. This was her game. She'd set the rules. Maybe she'd stopped playing and hadn't bothered to clue him in.

Elle introduced him to her guests. Some of them—like Dante and Tanner—he'd already met at Confidential Rejuvenations, but he didn't know Carlisle, Bridget, Brad or Sabrina.

"And last, but certainly not least, this is Julie DeMarco." With a flourish of her hand, Elle indicated Julie.

"We've met," Sebastian said.

"Oh, that's right," Elle said, feigning innocence. "I forgot."

Like hell, he thought.

Julie finally looked up.

They stared into each other's eyes, forks poised over their plates.

I know what you taste like. He telegraphed her the thought with his eyes.

She drilled him a look that said she was trying to gauge the depth of his soul. He noticed their chests were rising and falling in tandem as if inhaling and exhaling simultaneous breaths of air. There was such primal desire written on her face. The look was at once vulnerable and exceedingly tough.

It touched him, her naked strength.

He had an irresistible impulse to reach across the table and cup her cheek in his palm. If they hadn't been surrounded by people, he would have done just that. Only his awareness of his public image kept his hands on his fork and knife.

Her eyes rounded as if he had caressed her. As if she knew how much he wanted to kiss her. She was holding her breath. Intentionally trying not to match his rhythm now, he wondered?

If he were to finger the pulse at her throat would he discover her blood was pounding as fast as his own? Did she have any idea how much he hungered for her? What would she do if she knew that underneath the fancy napkin in his lap he was rock-hard for her?

"So tell us, Sebastian, how did you get into public relations?" Dante asked as he uncorked the bottle of wine Sebastian had brought and began pouring it for his guests. "Was it a family business?"

"No. PR came naturally to me," he said, never taking his eyes off Julie. "I'm a glass-half-full kind of guy and I've been told I have a talent for putting things in the most positive light."

"You must come across some very interesting things in your line of work," Elle said.

"No more than any of the rest of you, I'm sure. When you work with the public…" He trailed off, leaving his meaning open for interpretation.

Julie shot him a sly, seductive smile that snatched his breath from his lungs and made him ache to toss her over his shoulder like a Neanderthal and cart her back to his cave. Never mind that a handful of Confidential Rejuvenations' employees were witnesses.

He raked her over with his eyes.

Her cheeks pinked at his perusal. The sun had set and Dante had lit tiki torches. The flickering light cast shadows over her face. Her flaxen curls were pinned loosely to her head and a few long whispery wisps had escaped to float around her face. He pictured himself leaning across the table, pulling out those hairpins and watching the rest of the silky strands tumble around her shoulders.

Dangly sapphire earrings that matched the color of her eyes shone with a luminescent glow. He was close enough that he could see the hint of pink lace on her bra peeking below the V-neck of her sweater every time she leaned forward to spear a morsel of food. He remembered exactly what she looked like underneath her clothes and his throat tightened in response.

"How long have you been in business?" Vanessa asked.

"Since I got my MBA five years ago."

Dante filled Vanessa's glass then stepped over to tipple wine into Julie's, but she put her palm over it and shook her head. "I'm going to be leaving in a bit."

"So soon?" Elle said. "But it's not even late yet."

"I've had a long week." Julie was still looking at Sebastian, her blue eyes gleaming like glacier ice in the sun. Icy hot, sizzling, the image swallowing him whole.

"You can't tell us anything juicy about your clients?" Vanessa asked Sebastian.

He took a sip of wine. "I represent a very famous pop

star who's currently in a facility much like Confidential Rejuvenations."

"Courtney Sparks?" Tanner asked.

"No naming names," Sebastian said. "But I'm the reason she's in rehab instead of jail. I convinced the paparazzo who's foot she ran over that it was an accident."

"In other words," Julie said, "you lied."

He noted it was the first thing she'd said to him since he'd walked into Dante and Elle's backyard.

"No," he corrected. "I looked at all possible options and chose the one most favorable for my client."

"Face it," she said. "Your profession requires you to lie."

"Do you have a problem with the way I make a living?" he asked lightly, but inside he was battling some unexpected feelings. Irritation, surprise and a bit of bewilderment.

"Are you trying to pick a fight with me, Ms. DeMarco?" He narrowed his eyes. What *was* she so mad about?

"Who's up for more wine?" Dante asked, hopping up from his seat. "I've got more wine."

"The salad is delicious, Elle." Julie pushed back from the table. "I think I'll have seconds." She hurried over to the buffet table without a backward glance.

"It is good salad, Elle. I think I'll have seconds as well." Sebastian followed Julie.

When he reached the buffet table, he muscled in close to her. "What is your problem?" he demanded in a harsh whisper.

"My problem?" Her whisper was as angry as his.

"You're calling me a liar in front of your friends."

"Well, if the truth hurts…" She grabbed the thongs and smacked a bunch of romaine lettuce dotted with parmesan cheese onto her plate and drizzled Caesar dressing over it.

Her attitude was bothering the hell out of him. He shot

a glance over his shoulder, noticed that everyone was pretending to eat but they were really eavesdropping. "You're saying I lied to you?"

"Duh, yeah."

"Give me that." He took her plate and set it on the buffet table beside his, grabbed her by the elbow and pulled her around the side of the house.

She jerked her arm away from him. "Stop manhandling me."

"I'm not manhandling you, it's that I don't want all your friends to overhear our conversation."

Julie frowned. "Maybe you should have thought about that before you showed up here."

"Ah," he said, realization dawning. "That's why you're mad."

"We had a deal. Nothing but sex. No dating, nothing personal. You agreed and then you turn up here. That makes you a liar in my book."

"Um, I'm not the only one who's less than honest."

"I didn't lie to you."

"Yes, you did. You said you'd call me and you didn't. Why didn't you call me?"

She lifted her shoulder in a defensive gesture. "Why didn't you call me?"

He raised his palms. "You're the one with the complicated ground rules. I didn't want to risk breaking any of them. I didn't know you were going to be here. You didn't tell me."

Why did she have to look so damn cute while she was chewing him out? He couldn't get offended. Not when he wanted to kiss her so badly he couldn't stand it.

"You knew Elle and Dante were my friends."

"So I need to check with you before I accept dinner invitations from anyone who works at Confidential Rejuvenations?"

"That would be helpful, yes."

He threw back his head and laughed.

She scowled, crossed her arms over her chest. "What's so funny?"

"You."

She made an impatient noise. "I'm going back to my dinner." Julie started to flounce away, but he put out a restraining hand on her arm.

"You're trying too hard to dislike me," he said.

"Disliking you isn't hard at all."

"Now who's lying?"

"Let go of me."

Even turned partly away from him, he could see her nostrils flare. "What are you so afraid of, Jules?"

"Don't—" her voice cracked "—call me Jules."

"You don't like it?"

"That's what my friends call me."

"And I'm not good enough to be your friend, is that it?"

She drew in an audible breath. "Please, Sebastian, I'm doing the best I can."

He removed his hand and let her go then because he was feeling as shaky as her voice.

Julie hurried back to the table. Sebastian stood, watching her go, trying to figure out why he was provoking her.

He walked over to the gathering. Julie was picking up her purse, telling her friends she wasn't feeling well, that she was going home. He felt like a jerk for scaring her off and he was about to offer to walk her to her car when she scurried out the back gate.

Normally, he wouldn't have felt so out of place. He

would have made a joke, smoothed things over, but everyone at the picnic tables was staring at him. He felt guilty.

"Thanks for the lovely evening. The dinner was wonderful, you have a fabulous home," he told Dante and Elle.

"Ah, you're not leaving already?" Elle said, but he could tell she was only being polite. He knew her sympathies lay with Julie and he couldn't blame her.

"Got an early day tomorrow," he said.

There you go, lying again. Tomorrow was Saturday and he didn't have a damned thing to do.

He left the party, slipping out the back gate where Julie had just departed. And he saw her sitting in her car, parked at the curb, her head resting on the steering wheel. He walked over and tapped on her window.

She looked up at him and grudgingly rolled the window down.

"What's wrong?" he asked.

"My car won't start."

"You want me to drive you home?"

"That's okay." She fished her cell phone from her pocket. "I'll call a tow truck."

"I don't mind."

"Maybe I do."

"Okay," he said. "I'm not going to push myself on you." He was halfway to his car when she called to him.

"Sebastian."

He stopped, turned. "Yes, Julie?"

Her eyes looked sad and hopeful and confused, just like he felt. "I think it would be okay if you took me home."

7

NODDING, SEBASTIAN went back for her. He kept his face impassive. He didn't want her to see how excited he was.

He held the door open while she got out. Held it open again while she slipped into the passenger seat of his Mercedes. He touched her hand as she slid across the plush leather seats and immediately felt himself grow hard. No woman had ever made him this horny. He shut the door and went around to the driver's side.

Julie sat beside Sebastian as he drove away from Elle and Dante's quiet suburban neighborhood. Why the change of heart? Why had she decided to let him drive her home?

Women.

Who could understand them? Certainly not him. The inside of the car was so quiet all he could hear was the sound of their raggedy breathing.

"I want to apologize," she said. "For getting angry with you back there. I'm not mad at you. I'm mad at myself."

"What about?"

"I really don't want to get into it. I did something I'm not proud of and it's sort of coming back to haunt me."

"Does it have anything to do with me?"

"Sort of, but not really."

"Okay," he said. "If you don't want to talk about it, we won't talk about."

"It's not you."

"All right."

"It's me. I'm just..." She blew out her breath. Obviously something was upsetting her, but he wasn't going to pry. "I was just surprised to see you tonight."

"You weren't ever going to call me, were you?"

"No."

"Why not?"

"I don't know."

Surreptitiously, he watched her from the corner of his eye. Her skin looked translucent in the green dashboard light. Feminine power radiated from her every pore. She was so damned sexy. He thought about what he'd done to her in the stables on Sunday morning and he couldn't stop a smile from spreading across his face.

"What are you grinning about?" she asked. Apparently he wasn't the only one sending surreptitious glances.

"Wouldn't you like to know?" he teased.

"Yes, I would."

"I was thinking about you spread out in that hay—"

"Hang a left at the next street," she interrupted.

"But I thought you lived near Confidential Rejuvenations. That's in the opposite direction."

"I thought we might take a detour by the lake."

"Oh, yeah?"

"If you don't mind."

Mind? Why the hell would he mind a detour by the lake? He had a feeling she was up to something mischievous. Blood, heated and languid, pooled in his groin. Every nerve ending in his body jumped with excitement.

"Here, turn here."

He followed her directions as the road narrowed from

two lanes to one and the overgrowth of trees along the sides of the road thickened. A few minutes later, after passing numerous signs directing him, he spotted the lake shimmering silver in the moonlight.

After driving around a bit, he located a place to park overlooking the water. He hadn't been parking since he was a teenager taking his dates up on Mulholland Drive.

He killed the engine.

Julie got out.

Sebastian followed. She wandered to the water's edge and stood gazing out at the water. When he reached her, she turned and extended her hand toward him. He took it and she lead him across the open ground toward a small park.

It felt nice holding hands. In all his thirty years on earth he'd never really held hands with a woman. Not like this. Fingers interlaced, palms pressed together, feeling, really feeling her skin against his. He didn't want to let go and he was a little disappointed when she dropped his hand and wandered over to the swing set.

She plunked onto a swing and started a smooth back and forth motion. He sat on the swing next to her. He hadn't been on a swing in over twenty years. For several minutes they just swung together, saying nothing. Finally, Julie spoke. "My mom and dad used to bring me here when I was a little kid. We'd have a picnic lunch and they'd take turns pushing me on the swing."

"That qualifies as personal information," he pointed out, and then immediately wished he hadn't. He wanted to hear stories from her childhood.

"It does, doesn't it?"

"Hey, they're your rules, you know. You're free to break them if you want."

She kept swinging for a few minutes, pushing herself higher and higher, her beautiful blond hair trailing over her. Oddly enough, he got a lump in his throat watching her, picturing her as a child. She interrupted the silence and said, "No, it's a good rule. I'm not going to break it."

"Just to make us even, I'll tell you something about my childhood."

"You don't have to."

"When I was a kid, I wanted to be a rock star."

"You?"

"Yeah, that's what my old man said."

"Not the supportive type, your father?"

He waved a hand. "Never mind. That's not a good memory. I see why you have the rules. Sharing personal stories makes things too—"

"Personal," she finished for him. "I think we should stick with the sex."

"You're sure about that?"

"Lay down on the seesaw," she said.

"What?"

Her eyes gleamed impishly. "I have an idea and I give as good as I get, Sebastian Black. You got shortchanged on Sunday. Now stretch out on your back on the seesaw, put your butt in the middle so you're balanced."

"Um…" He had to admit he was intrigued. "Okay."

The seesaw was one of the old-fashioned wooden ones, but it had recently been sanded and repainted. He did as she asked, balancing himself on the seesaw.

"Reach over your head with both hands and grab onto the handle," she instructed.

"What are you up to?"

"Just do it."

"Or what?"

"Or you can take me home right now."

"Your bossiness is making me pretty damned hot."

"That's what I'm shooting for."

He reached up with both hands and took hold of the handle. "Now what?"

"Close your eyes."

"I'm a little apprehensive about this."

"I closed my eyes for you at the Sushi Palace."

"Yeah, but you knew all that I had up my sleeve was food. I have no idea—"

"Shh." She laid an index finger over his mouth. "Stop talking."

His gut was churning. The hairs on his arms were raised. His cock was steel. Hell, it was past steel. It was titanium.

She straddled the metal balance bar of the seesaw, scooted close to him and placed a palm on the flat of his stomach. Then she reached for the fly of his jeans. Sebastian hissed in air as she slowly dragged the zipper down.

The second the zipper was undone, his cock sprang free, jutting from his jeans like a periscope.

"You don't have any underwear on," she said, delighted.

"I was planning on doing laundry over the weekend."

Lightly, she stoked his head. "Mmm, you're so long and thick. I'm going to love taking you inside me."

Every muscle in his body tightened and he let out a stunted groan.

"Payback's a bitch, Mr. Black. I'll teach you to give me a tongue-lashing in the stables."

She touched the tip of her tongue to his throbbing head. "Mmm," she whispered again. "You taste as good as you look."

A low growl escaped his lips. There were so many things he wanted to tell her. How gorgeous she looked with her hair fanning about her face, how whenever he was with her he felt light-headed and a little breathless, how his spirits soared whenever she was near.

But the sentiments hung in his throat and he couldn't force them out. His brain was too far gone with the intensity of the pleasure she was plying.

JULIE GRINNED to herself, enjoying the power she wielded over him. He hadn't even tried to resist. He'd complied with everything she'd asked. Let him see what she'd experienced in the top of that hayloft when he'd run that hot tongue of his over her aching clit and drove her right out of her mind.

She kept one hand planted firmly on his abdomen and the other palm on his thighs, balancing the seesaw as she lowered her head between his legs.

His hard flesh filled her mouth as he swelled bigger and bigger still.

She swirled her tongue around him, at the same time moving her mouth up and down. It was a delicious dance, this primal rhythm. And as she sucked him, she gently rocked the seesaw back and forth, in tempo with what she was doing to his body.

He made hungry, desperate, guttural noises and she knew she was pleasing him. Returning the favor. Supplying him the same sweet bliss he'd given her in the hayloft the previous weekend.

His shaft kept growing, expanding, thickening until she feared it would no longer fit in her mouth. The tip engorged with blood. It pulsed hot against her lips.

He groaned.

Was she hurting him?

Julie pulled back.

"No," he said in a strangled cry and grasped her hair in his fingers. "Don't stop."

She could feel his entire body quivering and that touched her in a way she could not define or describe. In that one precious moment in time, he belonged totally to her and Julie reveled in the feeling.

His fingers moved from her hair to her face, his strokes light as butterfly wings.

She kept it up. Taking him into her mouth, letting him almost slide all the way out before inhaling him again, all the while rocking the seesaw.

He let out a cry, part anguish, part rapture. The sound startled and pleased her at the same time.

And then suddenly, she had him.

His orgasm blasted through him, an explosion of release, and he spilled into Julie's welcoming mouth, heated and coppery.

Yes, yes, I want all of you.

Julie swallowed, delicately licked her lips, and rested her face against his pelvis. She could hear the sound of her blood pumping hotly through her ears.

Sebastian dropped his legs off the seesaw and the plank sank to the ground. He took her into his arms, pulled her up tight against him. The seesaw teetered shakily.

"That was…you were…" He was too breathless to finish the sentence.

"Shh."

"I love…"

What? His words sent a blast of alarm through her. She

didn't want to hear this. It was one thing to have an affair with a notorious playboy, it was quite another to find out he was falling in love with you.

"I love what you did to my body," he finished. "That was awesome. You're awesome."

Relief shagged her shoulders while simultaneously she felt strangely disappointed. What the heck was the matter with her? She didn't want him to be in love with her. She didn't want to be in love with him. It wasn't love. It was just chemistry and phenomenal sex. Love had nothing to do with it.

Right?

He pulled back from her a bit, cupped her chin in his palm, raised her face up to meet his eyes. "You okay?"

"I'm fine." She forced a smile and tucked her doubts and fears to the back of her mind.

Sebastian pulled her closer until they were straddling the middle of the seesaw together. It rose up, rocked. He kissed her lightly, carefully balancing them on the precarious fulcrum.

Julie couldn't help thinking that one wrong move and they'd both come crashing down hard.

ABSENTMINDEDLY, Julie made change-of-shift rounds on her patients, checking on them before the afternoon therapy sessions began. As a counselor in training, Confidential Rejuvenations allowed her to moderate group meetings under the supervision of a certified sex therapist.

Saturday sessions tended to be the most emotionally intense and it was the reason Julie often volunteered to work the weekend shifts so she could learn more. Normally, she looked forward to her work, but today all she wanted to do was daydream about Sebastian.

Snap out of it, DeMarco. Your patients are depending on your levelheadedness.

But no matter how hard she tried to stay focused, she often found herself staring off into space remembering exactly how great it felt to be held in Sebastian's arms.

He'd driven her home after the park, walked her to the front porch and kissed her good-night. Then this morning she'd awakened to find her car parked in her driveway. She didn't know how he'd managed it, but somehow he'd got her car running and he'd left her a cute little note propped against the steering wheel for her to find. It left her feeling all mushy inside.

She slipped the card from her pocket and took another look at it. On the front was a big yellow smiley face, on the blank page inside he'd written a simple message.

Good morning, sunshine. Had your car fixed. Hope you slept well. Thanks for last night,
Sebastian.

Looking at the card made her feel like sunshine. Smiling, she stuck it back into her pocket.

"Somebody must have had a good night last night," Maxine said as Julie drifted dreamily past the nurses' station. "It's too bad that today is lining up to be a doozy."

"Oh?"

"You're getting a new patient." Maxine slapped the patient notification summary on the desk in front of her, then lowered her voice. "It's the actor Colin Cruz. He was in town filming a movie and apparently there's a juicy scandal to go with it, but I don't have the details. Maybe you'll get it out of him in group."

"And if I do, you'll never know about it," Julie replied. "We are called *Confidential* Rejuvenations for a good reason."

"You're so bad at gossip," Maxine teased.

Any other day she might have gotten flustered at the thought of having Colin Cruz, one of the most handsome young movie stars in the business, as her patient, but today the only one who flustered her mind was Sebastian.

"Cruz is going by the name Joe Anderson," Maxine continued. "He's down in admitting right now. Dr. Carpenter's already added him to this evening's group session."

"Thanks for the information." Julie scooped up the notification summary and headed down the corridor to get ready for her illustrious new patient.

Fifteen minutes later Colin Cruz arrived on the floor, dressed all in black, wearing designer sunglasses and flanked by bodyguards. A thin, well-dressed gray-haired woman hurried along beside him. Heads swiveled as he went by and whispers rippled in his wake.

Julie escorted him to his room and recited the hospital rules and regulations. The actor never spoke a word. Instead, he stretched out on the bed with his shoes on and flipped on the television set. The gray-haired woman turned out to be his executive assistant, and she answered all of Julie's questions about Colin's medical history.

"Your first group session starts at six o'clock this evening," Julie told Colin.

He grunted. He still had the sunglasses on so she couldn't see if he was looking at her or not.

"You're expected to be there," she said firmly. The people who were admitted to the sexual dysfunction unit were almost always in crisis. Most often, they had hit bottom and were forced to admit their sexual behavior was out of control.

Julie thought about last night and swallowed. Was she on the verge of some kind of sexual addiction herself? Was that why she couldn't stop thinking about Sebastian?

It was a disturbing thought. She'd seen firsthand how out-of-control sexual addictions and deviant sexual behavior could mess up promising lives.

Come on, you're not a sex addict, nor are you a sexual deviant. Not according to the wild stories she heard in group. In fact, she was the opposite. Tame and dull and…

Oh, yeah? Who's been having wild romps in the stable hayloft and a park by the lake at midnight?

Julie batted back the thoughts and finished getting the uncooperative Mr. Cruz ensconced in his room. Then she went to get a look at the physician's admission orders that Maxine was in the process of inputting into the computer.

"By the way," Maxine said, as Julie stood reading the orders over her shoulder. "Devi Parker is running late. She said you should start the six o'clock session without her."

"She's letting me start the session?" Julie asked, feeling excited. She'd never run a session without a supervisor in the room. This was her chance to show her mentor she could handle the group on her own.

"She's only going to be five or ten minutes late, don't get your hopes up," Maxine said. "You won't be getting your own group until you pass that exam."

"Thanks for reminding me," she mumbled.

Maxine smirked. "Hey, what are colleagues for?"

At six o'clock, Julie assembled the group in the meeting room, which had no windows to ensure complete privacy. The door also locked from the inside so no one could walk in on a session in progress. A red light over the door signaled to the staff when a session was taking place.

There were usually six to ten members in a group and the chairs were arranged in a circle without a table to interrupt the flow of conversation.

With the addition of Colin Cruz, this group was full. Julie sat in the circle with them, an empty chair to her left for Devi when she arrived. "The therapist is going to be a bit late today but she told me to go ahead and start the session. She'll be joining us shortly. Everyone, as you can see we have a new patient in group today. Please welcome Joe Anderson."

"He looks like Colin Cruz to me," one of the male patients muttered. He was a sullen nineteen-year-old dressed in Goth attire with multiple piercings in odd places.

"It's Confidential Rejuvenations' policy never to violate anyone's privacy. This is Joe Anderson, just like you're Mike Brown," Julie said. She turned to the young woman on her right. The girl had been at Confidential Rejuvenations for a couple of weeks and was making great progress in conquering her sexual need to dress like a bunny rabbit and rub up against people in a lewd manner. "Amanda, would you like to start?"

"So what'd you do, *Joe?*" Mike asked Colin Cruz with an upward jerk of his pierced chin. "Banged the wrong starlet? Is she some producer's underage daughter or something? And now you're off his movie set if you don't go to sex rehab?"

"Mike," Julie admonished the young man whose own father was a country-and-western chart-topping multimillionaire musician. Mike had been sent to Confidential Rejuvenations after being caught making and distributing tapes on the Internet of himself having sex with sixteen-year-old triplets. "You're way out of line."

Before Julie had time to react, Colin Cruz jerked his foot underneath the leg of Mike's chair and tipped it over to upend the young man on his butt.

Colin leapt to his feet, put a boot to Mike's throat and stared down at him. "You wanna know what I did?"

Mike's eyes widened and he shook his head.

The pulse in Julie's throat jumped. "Joe," she said as sternly as she could. "Please take your seat."

Colin ignored her. "I screwed a mobster's wife while he was in the next room taking a nap. See, I got a thing for danger. It freakin' turns me on."

Mike was making choking noises.

"Joe!" Julie demanded. "Sit down now or I'll call security."

Hit the panic button, her instincts cried and she shot a glance at the red alarm button on the wall by the door.

But she didn't want to do that. It was her first time leading the group alone. She'd be the laughingstock of the floor if she couldn't handle a simple altercation between the patients.

"Dude," one of the other group members, a lanky professional skateboarder said. "We're being broadcast on the Web."

Colin's head jerked up and his eyes narrowed to slits at the skateboarder. "What are you talking about?"

The skateboarder held up his cell phone. "My friend just texted me. We're live, dude. There's a camera in this room."

Slowly, Colin lifted his boot from Mike's throat and stalked toward Julie.

He's going to kill me.

Julie sprang to her feet, headed for the panic button.

"Where is it?" he demanded, placing himself between her and the panic button. "Where's the camera"

"I don't know what you're talking about."

"You set me up."

"I didn't," she denied.

That's when she saw the switchblade in his hand.

AFTER HIS LATE-NIGHT tryst in the park with Julie, everything changed for Sebastian. He tackled the campaign with new vigor, determined to put in place the approved public relations plan so that it couldn't fail to pull Confidential Rejuvenations' reputation out of the skids.

That morning he'd gotten up earlier and had Julie's car towed. He'd lavishly tipped the mechanic to put a rush on it and then he'd driven it to her condo, parked in the driveway and taken a cab to his hotel. He'd spent the rest of the day working on the computer, putting together a spreadsheet timeline of all the odd occurrences that had been attributed to the saboteur.

Part of him had hoped Julie would call when she got the little card he'd left her, but she hadn't. It was okay. He'd give her space, let her come to him in her own time.

Finally, after hours of work, he stopped to take a break and order room service. He'd just bitten into a French-dip sandwich when his cell phone rang. He swallowed, dabbed at his mouth with a napkin and picked up the phone. "Hello?"

"Black?"

"Yes, sir," he said, coming to attention at the sound of Dr. Jarrod Butler's voice.

"We've got a problem."

Tucking the phone against his chin, he scrambled to his feet. "What is it?"

"There's been an incident here at the hospital and the place is crawling with media. We need a spokesman to deal with the upheaval."

Sebastian jammed his feet into his shoes and rolled down the sleeves of his dress shirt. "Could you be a bit more specific?"

"I'll explain everything when you get here."

"I'm on my way," he said, but Butler had already hung up, leaving him talking to a dial tone.

Sebastian's mind conjured up a hundred different possibilities as he zoomed through the Saturday-evening traffic in his rented red Mercedes. What could have happened to cause such tension in Dr. Butler's voice?

Ten minutes later, he reached the security gates of Confidential Rejuvenations to witness a cadre of media vans parked along the sides of the road. Camera crews hung about and he spied a couple of intrepid reporters trying to scale the eight-foot-high privacy fence erected around the grounds. Armed security guards with their hands on the butts of their gun holsters were shouting at them to get down or they'd be arrested for criminal trespassing.

The security guard at the gate recognized Sebastian and let him through while two other security guards held the surge of paparazzi at bay.

The parking lot was a hodgepodge of haphazardly parked cars. He quickly spied Butler and Covey and Senator Robert Garcia, along with Tanner Doyle and a fortysomething woman in a white lab coat that he'd never met before, conferring outside the doctors' entrance to the hospital.

Sebastian trotted over.

"Thank God you're here," William Covey said and clapped him on the back.

Jarrod Butler shoved his hands through his thinning hair. "This is a PR nightmare."

"What's going down?" Sebastian asked, his body strumming with adrenaline. These were the moments he lived for. Swooping in, saving the day.

"Colin Cruz has taken a roomful of sex addicts hostage," Robert Garcia supplied.

Sebastian swung his gaze to the senator. It wasn't a statement he ever thought he'd hear. It sounded so comical that he almost smiled. But from the looks on their faces this wasn't the time or place for levity.

"Colin Cruz, the actor?"

"Yes, you know. *Four Guns of Calderone, Minnie and Steve, Last Train to Pittsburgh.* He won an Oscar for his role as hit man Handy Andy in *Last Train to Pittsburgh,*" said Dr. Covey, who clearly kept abreast of movies.

Sebastian knew who Colin was. The studly young actor lived not far from his home in Beverly Hills. He'd even seen Colin in the organic foods market shopping for vegan fare. "How did this come about?"

"It's my fault," said the woman, who extended her hand to Sebastian. "I'm Devi Parker, the therapist in charge. I was late and I told the nurse who normally assists me to go ahead and begin the session. She's very competent, even though she doesn't yet have her certification. But I didn't know Colin Cruz had just joined us or I never would have allowed her to start group with an unknown entity."

Dr. Butler glanced over his shoulder and stuffed his hands into his pockets. "Let's talk in Tanner's office."

They trooped inside and reconvened in the security

office, which was housed in the hospital basement safely out of earshot of the paparazzi.

"Have you notified the police?" Sebastian asked Tanner.

Tanner shook his head and shot a glance at Butler, Covey and Garcia. "They wanted me to wait, but I think we're in over our heads and we need a hostage negotiator."

Sebastian settled himself on the corner of Tanner's desk. "That's good that you didn't call the authorities. If we can keep the cops out of it I might be able to turn this whole thing around."

"Are you trained at hostage negotiation?" Tanner's tone was sarcastic.

"If you let me do my job, there will be no need for hostage negotiation," Sebastian said smoothly, a smile affixed to his face. He was accustomed to this sort of reaction. He didn't take it personally. "Now tell me exactly what transpired."

"Julie DeMarco was leading a group session for sex addicts. Colin Cruz was admitted this afternoon for treatment and it was his first time in group," Dr. Butler explained. "We had no idea he was so volatile."

"Julie." Her name escaped Sebastian lips without him even being aware he'd spoken. At the mention of her name his stomach torqued and all the moisture drained from his mouth.

"That's right. At some point during the first few minutes of the session, Colin took Julie and the nine other people in the room as hostages."

Sebastian's breath stilled in his lungs and he felt as if he'd just been kicked in the gut. "Does he have a gun?"

"He has a knife," Tanner said.

Sebastian crossed his arms over his chest and tried to appear calm and fully in control, when he was feeling anything but calm and controlled. He wanted to wrap his hands around that son-of-a-bitch Cruz and throttle him. If he harmed one hair on Julie's head…

Easy, easy. You can solve this with sweet talk. You're the best at it.

"How do you know all this?" he asked Tanner.

Tanner's eyes met Sebastian's. "That's the thing. Someone had a camera installed inside the conference room. It was turned on and broadcasting the session via live stream through the hospital's Wi-Fi Internet connect. Colin Cruz's private confessions of his sex addiction went straight to the World Wide Web."

"Someone installed a camera in the session room?"

"It must be the saboteur," Dr. Butler guessed.

Tanner clasped his hands behind his back and paced the small piece of ground in front of his desk. "When Colin realized what was happening, he freaked out. He thought he'd been set up by someone at the hospital. He took the room hostage, and then destroyed the camera so we can no longer see what's going on in there."

"Has he made any demands?"

"We haven't tried negotiating with him. We didn't get that far. He's too upset and the place was besieged with paparazzi within minutes of the session being aired on the Internet."

A sudden calm settled over Sebastian. He had his emotions under wraps. He slid off Tanner's desk. "It's in the bag."

"What do you mean?" Tanner asked.

The head of security was a good three inches taller than his own six-foot height, but Sebastian wasn't going to let the man intimidate him.

"Just take me to Cruz."

8

UP ON THE FIFTH FLOOR, Julie was trying her best to talk sense into Colin. She'd stopped calling him Joe Anderson because at this point, all anonymity was lost and he responded better to his real name.

After the skateboarder's friend sent him a text message saying their therapy session was all over the Internet, Colin had paced the room, searching for the Web camera until he'd found it embedded into the wall behind the seascape.

That threw Colin into a tailspin. He was paranoid and sweating, terrified the mobster whose wife he'd slept with would hear about the Internet stream. He'd made everyone sit with their backs against the wall while he paced and ranted and waved the knife around. Julie had spent the last hour and a half speaking calmly, reasonably, reassuring him that as long as he let everyone go unharmed everything could be resolved.

Colin was beginning to settle down and she almost had him convinced to give her the knife, when the skateboarder got another text message.

"Dude," the skateboarder said, "my buddy says paparazzi are swarming the hospital."

Colin let loose with a fresh string of curses.

"Give me that." Julie got up and snatched the cell phone out of the guy's hand. "You're agitating him."

"Hey!"

"Hush. You sit there and be quiet."

Colin pointed the knife at her. "You be quiet, too, and sit back down. All of you shut up and let me think."

But Julie didn't sit back down. She stood her ground, held out her hand. "Give me the knife, Colin. You know you don't want any more trouble. This can end right here. All you have to do is hand me the knife and we'll all walk out of here. I'll explain to Dr. Carpenter what happened. I'll intervene on your behalf."

"I'm screwed. My career is over."

"No, no, it's not. You can turn your life around. You can be a role model." She took a step toward him.

His hand was shaking and his eyes looked so desperate.

"That's it. That's right. Give me the knife." She took another step and then another. "You look so tired, Colin. Like you've been carrying the weight of the world on your shoulders. It's okay to lay your burden down. We're here to help you."

Colin's eyes misted with tears but he blinked them back.

"That's it," she soothed as if she were cooing to her hamster, Felix. "I know you don't want to hurt anyone. I know you're a good person."

"I don't want to hurt anyone." Colin was shaking his head.

"You just need help."

"I do, I need help." His voice cracked.

"Please, please, give me the knife and we'll fix this." Almost there. One more step.

Colin extended his hand. He was about to pass her the knife.

And then Sebastian Black knocked on the door and ruined everything.

TANNER HAD LED the procession from the basement office to the elevator to the sexual dysfunction unit on the fifth floor. They'd walked down the corridor, headed for the therapy room that was flanked by two armed security guards and Colin Cruz's physician. Tanner nodded and the guards stepped aside.

Sebastian had approached and knocked on the door and called out, "Colin, Sebastian Black here."

There was a long moment of silence and then Colin said, "Sebastian Black, the publicist?"

"Yes."

"Go away, Black, you're as bad as an ambulance chaser." Colin's voice was high and reedy. The voice of a man on the edge. He was dangerous and Julie was in that room with him.

Hang on to all your bravado. Don't get distracted. You can talk him down.

Sebastian let out a hearty laugh. "You can let go of the role now, Colin. I know you're a dedicated actor and that you believe in staying in character at all times when preparing for an upcoming part. But I think the good people here at Confidential Rejuvenations might have misunderstood our intention."

"Huh?"

"Now's the time to come on out and tell the press that you're not really a sex addict. That this was all prep for your upcoming movie about a sex addict who takes his therapy group hostage. And I'll confess that little bit of theatrics with the camera and the Internet stuff was nothing more than my idea of a publicity stunt. It's all my fault. Not all my ideas are good ones."

"Yeah..." Colin's reply was muffled by the door, but Sebastian could hear the relief in the young actor's tone. "Stupid idea, Black."

"Open the door, shake everyone's hand, no hard feelings and you and I will go out to meet the media together."

A moment passed.

"Colin?"

The door cracked open and Colin Cruz emerged, face flushed, hair mussed, but mercifully empty-handed.

"Damn." Sebastian heard one of the security guards whisper to the other. "He's good."

But Sebastian was already looking past Colin into the room, his eyes searching for only one person.

Julie's eyes met his. In her hand, she gingerly held the switchblade knife Colin had used to hold the room hostage. The minute he saw her, he started breathing again and it was only then did he realize he'd been holding his breath.

She was all right. Relief left him weak.

Everyone else rushed out, pushing past Julie and Colin and Sebastian, scattering down the hallway, heading back to the safety of their rooms.

"Dude," Colin said, in a low shaky voice, "you're a genius."

"I charge like one, too."

"You saved my reputation."

"All in a day's work." Sebastian shook the young actor's hand. "Give me a second and I'll escort you to our press conference."

Sebastian walked past Colin and went straight to Julie. She tilted her chin up. He expected her to fall into his arms. Or at the every least give him a grateful smile, and a heart-felt thank-you.

But he didn't get any of those things.

Arms akimbo, Julie glared at him.

"Are you okay?" he asked. He was desperate to touch her but he could tell that was the last thing she wanted.

"Jackass," she muttered and passed the knife to Tanner, who'd followed Sebastian into the room.

"Excuse me."

"You heard me. You're a jackass."

He couldn't have been more stunned if she'd hauled off and slapped him across the face. Sebastian took her by the shoulders. "Wait a minute."

She twisted away from him. "Hands off," she hissed.

"What am I missing here? I just saved your life and the lives of nine other people and you're calling me a jackass? Wanna clue me in?"

"Because now, thanks to you and your publicity stunt scheme, that young man—who is deeply troubled by the way—isn't going to get the help he so desperately needs."

"Huh?"

Julie pointed to where Colin stood in the corridor waiting for Sebastian. "Do you seriously think he's going to stay in therapy now?"

He couldn't believe she was blaming him when he'd been the one to rescue her. He'd expected her to look at him as if he were some action hero. A knight slaying her dragons. Prince Charming squiring Cinderella at the ball. Instead, she was looking at him as if he had leprosy.

Sebastian wasn't used to that. Nor was he accustomed to what he was feeling. Tenderness, affection, apprehension, guilt. What he'd wanted to do—what he'd had to fist his hands to keep from doing—was to lift her in his arms, take her back to his hotel room, slowly strip off her clothes and make love to her all night long.

"Hey, the cow was already out of the barn because of that

video camera hooked up to the Web," he said, unnerved by what he was feeling and falling back on flippancy. "I was only trying to defuse an explosive situation and it worked."

"No, what you did is feed into Colin's fantasy that he has the right to do whatever he wants when things don't suit him. I had it under control. I was talking him down, but did you even bother to assess the situation before you so cavalierly offered your solution?" She looked mad enough to spit fire.

Sebastian took a step back. He would never have believed Julie was capable of such a passionate outburst. And against him. She was livid.

"We'll talk about this later," he said.

"Don't bother," she retorted and stormed off with a toss of her head.

Sebastian turned to Tanner. "Was I out of line in any way?"

Tanner shrugged. "She's medical personnel. They have a different way of looking at things. My fiancée, Vanessa, and I have had to work through a few differences of opinion like this. Give her time. She'll come around."

"I don't have the time and I don't need her to come around. I barely know her."

"You might not know her very well, but she's got your number." Tanner chuckled.

What the hell? Since when had he been become the butt of everyone's joke?

Colin Cruz was out in the hallway nervously shifting from foot to foot. Sebastian went to join him. "You really think you can convince them it was all a stunt for a movie role?" he asked.

"I got you to let your hostages go, didn't I?" Sebastian straightened his sleeves beneath his jacket, tightened his tie and then ran a hand through his hair.

Julie might be mad at him, but it didn't matter. He'd

done what he'd been hired to do. Make a bad situation look good. It's what he did best.

"Come on, Cruz," he said and headed for the elevator. "Let's spin this thing."

DR. BUTLER SENT Julie home early. She didn't want to go, but he insisted, saying she'd been through a scary ordeal and needed time to process what had happened.

She suspected the truth was the chief of staff wanted her out of the way of the media so Sebastian could do his spin-doctoring without her mucking things up for him. She was still furious over his interference.

"I was handling it," she told her hamster, Felix, as she sat on her sofa with her feet—shod in fluffy pink socks—propped up on the coffee table. A nighttime drama played on the television, but she had the sound muted. She'd started watching the program to distract herself, but quickly lost interest. Today, her own life had been a regular soap opera. She didn't need any more drama.

Felix sat in her lap, busily gnawing a carrot.

"I totally had it under control. Sure, I was scared when Colin found that camera and the skateboarder got that text from a friend that our session was on the Web. And then when Colin flipped out and pulled the switchblade from his pocket, I did get a little panicky. But who wouldn't?"

Felix blinked.

"Oh, you think that now. You're here and safe and warm, but in the heat of the moment, you never know what you'll do."

Great. Here she was talking to a hamster as if he was a person. Felix polished off the rest of the carrot and ran up her arm to sit on her shoulder.

"I'm sure it must have looked like he took us hostage.

He was waving the knife around and saying stupid things, but really, we were never in any actual danger."

Felix made a sympathetic hamster noise.

"I'd almost talked him into putting the knife down and walking out of the room when that irritating Sebastian Black interfered. He's so smooth and glib and cocky and…ooh, ooh, there he is on TV."

The television program had given way to the ten o'clock news and there was Sebastian in all his peacock glory. Julie reached for the remote and pumped up the volume.

The anchorman smiled at the camera. "A scary incident at Confidential Rejuvenations—a facility that has suffered more than its share of bad publicity of late—was the scene of what was at first mistakenly believed to have been a hostage situation involving star actor Colin Cruz."

The camera switched to Sebastian, who was being interviewed outside Confidential Rejuvenations. He reiterated his lie that Mr. Cruz had merely been deeply immersed in his character of a sex addict for a new film role and the leak of his *therapy* session was nothing more than a publicity stunt.

Julie ground her teeth and threw the remote at the screen. It fell harmlessly short of the television set, hitting the carpet with a soft bounce. "Liar, liar, pants on fire."

Felix quivered on her shoulder. He hated loud noises.

"Sorry," she whispered, then scooped him up and put him back in his cage, just as the doorbell chimed.

Julie padded to the door and stood on tiptoes to peer through the peephole. She saw Sebastian lounging insouciantly against the column on her front porch.

She jerked opened the door. "What the hell do you want?"

"Good evening to you, too, Julie."

"I saw you on TV. Looking as vainglorious as ever."

He lifted an eyebrow. "Vainglorious?"

"It means conceited. Look it up. Good night." She reached back to close the door, but he quickly stepped across the threshold.

"You're not getting rid of me that easily." He strolled past her. For the first time, she noticed he carried a paper bag. "I brought wine. I hope you like red. We're going to have a glass and hash this out."

She followed him into her kitchen. "There's no reason for us to hash anything out."

"Yes there is. You're mad at me and I don't like it when people are mad at me." He started opening drawers.

"Then stop doing things that make people mad at you. Like coming into their homes uninvited and rifling through their cabinets."

"Where do you keep the corkscrew?"

"Fourth drawer on your left." Why was she telling him this? Why wasn't she throwing him out of her apartment?

Because she was *glad* to see him. How could she both dislike him and want him so desperately at the same time? It was confusing.

He found the corkscrew, unpeeled the foil from the neck of the wine bottle and plunged the tool inside the cork, twisting with a smooth, practiced motion that told her he'd opened many bottles of wine in his lifetime. She found herself fascinated by his broad palms, neatly trimmed fingernails and muscular wrist.

The cork came out with a soft pop.

Julie gulped.

"Wineglasses?"

She turned to the cabinet to keep from looking at him, took

out two wineglasses and passed them to him. He measured out a generous serving of Pinot Noir. "Let's sit down."

"How do you know you're not interrupting me in the middle of something?"

"You were watching the news."

"How do you know I wasn't making out with my lover?" she asked. "How do you know he's not in the bedroom getting his gun to come in here and shoot you?"

He looked completely unruffled. "Do you have a gun-wielding lover?"

She glowered. "No."

His familiar smirk lifted the corners of his mouth. "Then let's sit."

God, but he was infuriating.

He headed toward the living room without waiting for her to follow. "Hey, you've got a hamster." He set the wine-glasses down on the coffee table, then walked over to admire Felix in his habitat. "I used to have hamsters when I was a kid. And rabbits and goats and pigs and—"

"You?" She picked up one of the wineglasses and took a courage-bolstering swig.

"Yeah, me."

She eyed him. From the top of his expensively clipped hair to the bottom of his polished Italian leather shoes. "You don't look like a farm boy."

"Commune."

"Huh?"

"It was more than a farm. I was raised on a commune."

"Seriously?"

"I am from California," he said. "I did it all. Slopped hogs, mucked stalls, milked cows."

"I can't see that."

"It happened and I really don't want for it to ever happen again."

"So you're one of those rebellious I'm-going-opposite-the-way-I-was-raised types?"

His grin widened and he sauntered back across the room toward her. "I suppose I am. How 'bout you?"

"How 'bout me what?" Julie stood her ground, even though she wanted to back up and put more distance between them.

His gaze traveled over her, his dark eyes gleaming. "Are you rebellious or a conformer?"

"I used to be a conformer," she admitted, "but then a few things happened that showed me the error of my ways. I'm giving 'rebel' an honest shot."

"Ah, that explains it."

"Explains what?"

"The whole, I-wanna-be-a-bad-girl thing."

She thought of Roger. "I have done some bad things."

"I seriously doubt that."

"You'd be surprised."

"Yeah?" He stepped closer, wineglass held loosely in his hand. "How so?"

She didn't mean to tell, but the look in his eyes and the need to let him know she wasn't as sweet and innocent as he thought pushed the admission out of her. "I had an affair with a married man."

"You?"

Her confession had the desired effect. He looked shocked and oddly jealous.

"I'm not proud of it."

"Still." He made a noise of disbelief. "I can't wrap my head around that information. Not in regards to you."

"I didn't know he was married at the time and I broke it

off the minute I found out, but I should have seen the signs. Weeknights, my calls always went to voice mail and we could never be together on the weekends. I was just so head over heels, I didn't want to think about it."

The disappointment she saw in his eyes hurt more than she could ever imagine. She was never going to let him know that his brother's future father-in-law was the married man she had an affair with.

"I thought we weren't supposed to talk about personal stuff," he said lightly.

She gave him a grateful smile and sat down.

Sebastian followed, sinking onto the sofa cushion beside her. "Instead," he said, "let's talk about what happened tonight. We need to get this sorted out between us."

She tensed and took a sip of wine. It was very good. She had to hand it to him. The man had excellent taste.

"Honestly, Jules, I didn't mean to step on your toes," he said. "I was simply trying to save face for Confidential Rejuvenations and Colin Cruz. I was doing my job."

She pushed a strand of hair behind one ear. "Without any consideration for the consequences?"

He shrugged and settled back against the couch. "In my book it was a win-win situation."

"Colin checked himself out of rehab."

"He didn't have a choice."

"Because you gave him an easy out."

"There's an easy solution. He can do private one-on-one sessions with a doctor."

He rested his right foot on his left lower thigh and balanced his wineglass on his right knee, his index finger and thumb lightly gripping the stem of the glass. All they needed for a seduction was a roaring fire and sexy music.

Her gaze fixed on the thickness of his fingers and her breathing quickened. "Julie."

"Yes?"

"You've got to understand my position."

"Colin has an addiction to sex and he's going to get in serious trouble. Who'll be there to bail him out the next time something like this happens? And unless he gets treatment, something like this will happen again."

"I'll be there to bail him out." Sebastian smiled. "He hired me as his publicist."

"You don't get it, do you?" Julie huffed. "A one-on-one session with a doctor isn't as effective as group therapy. You're putting Colin's image—and the money he makes for the people who invest in his image—over his well-being. Where did you get such skewed values? From the commune? Or from rebelling against it?"

Sebastian looked genuinely puzzled and that was the hell of it—the man didn't see anything wrong with putting style over substance. He was so into the Beverly Hills lifestyle he couldn't see beyond his own nose.

"I do want to apologize if I've upset you."

"Is this a true apology?" she asked. "Or is it one of your PR apologies, manufactured to get what you want?"

His eyes met hers. "And what do I want?"

"You want to get me into bed again."

He laughed. "We've never been in a bed together, Jules."

Julie took a big gulp, draining the rest of her wine. The man bedeviled her and she had no idea how to handle her muddled feelings toward him. "Then why are you here?"

"I told you. I don't want you to be mad at me."

"Why do you care?"

"Honestly, I don't know."

That gave her pause. For the life of her, she couldn't figure him out. One minute she thought he was just a glib, arrogant playboy and then out of the blue, he'd get this look of abject longing on his face. A look that said he'd missed out on something important and he didn't know how to fill the empty hole in his life.

Of course, if she were to say this to him, she had no doubt he would merely laugh at her attempts to psychoanalyze him. She didn't know why she was even trying to figure him out.

"You confuse me," Sebastian said, voicing her very thoughts about him. He set his glass on the coffee table and leaned closer to her.

"How so?" she whispered, struck by how much she wanted him to kiss her and her fear that if he did, she wouldn't be able to stop kissing him.

"You're sweet and innocent on the outside, but tough on the inside. How'd you get so tough? You have brothers?"

"Only child," she said, her gaze hooking on his lips. The man had gorgeous lips. Full and wide and well-defined. There were women who'd kill for lips like those.

"You should be spoiled rotten, but you're not," he said. "More paradox."

"My dad died when I was fourteen. I had to grow up fast." She shouldn't be telling him this. She didn't want to tell him anything about her personal life. Why was she telling him this?

"My mom died when I was ten," he continued.

"Is this a 'poor me' contest?" she asked, trying to steer the conversation away from their past. "One-upping each other to see who had the saddest childhood?"

"If it was," he said smoothly, "I guarantee I'd win. But I

don't let the past define who I am. I'm a self-made man. I take all the credit and I accept all the blame for who I am."

She did admire that quality in him. As a nurse in a rehabilitation setting, most people she ran across were looking for someone to blame for their problems. It took a lot of hard work in therapy to get them to realize that more often than not, the person in the mirror was the source of their problems.

"You told me you had a brother. Any other siblings?" she asked.

"Linc's my half brother. Same mother, different fathers. No other siblings."

"Did you and Linc grow up together?"

"We did."

"Is your brother older or younger?"

"Linc's five years younger."

"Are you two close?"

"We are. Were."

"You guys have a falling-out?" She leaned back against the couch and studied him. She was feeling nice and fluid from the wine and she couldn't remember why she was mad at him. He was too darned cute to stay mad at.

No, not cute. This guy was seriously handsome. He was so damned handsome, her chest tightened.

He stretched an arm around the back of the couch. She could feel him, even though he wasn't quite touching her. Heat radiated off his body, washing over her in waves.

"I don't like his fiancée."

"Roger Marshall's daughter."

"Yeah."

"Why don't you like her?" Julie asked. She felt odd about

Roger's daughter. Because they were fairly close in age, she couldn't help wondering how his daughter would feel if she learned her father had had an affair with a woman near her own age. The thought made her sick to her stomach. "Is she a bad person?"

"No." He inched closer.

Julie focused on Sebastian's lips in order to keep from thinking about Roger's daughter and how hurt she'd be if she knew about the affair. "Does she have bad habits?"

"Not really. She's obnoxious about recycling."

"So what's the problem?"

"She's too opinionated."

"Oh, so she's too much like you."

Sebastian frowned. "She's not like me at all. I just think she's not the right one for Linc."

"Is that true? Or is it that you don't like that she's taking him away from you?"

Julie could tell she'd hit bone. Sebastian's eyelids lowered and he assessed her for a long moment. "I think you ask too many questions," he said. "You're pesky that way."

"Maybe you don't ask enough questions."

"What can I say? I'm a shallow guy."

"Honestly?" She pressed a palm to her chest. "I would never have guessed."

"Sarcasm. Cute."

He moved closer still and Julie didn't retreat. She was tipsy on wine and his handsomeness. He hovered mere inches from her mouth now. He looked like every fairy-tale prince ever written about. She inhaled his intoxicating scent, which was a combination of rich red grapes, the citrusy hint of bergamot and the lively tang of spearmint.

9

HIS KISS SPUN HER around and turned her upside down.

The other kisses he'd given her were nothing like this. Those kisses had been sensational, sure.

But this kiss…

This kiss!

It was like a kept promise. It was the ultimate summer vacation. It was the longed-for Christmas gift. It was the opposite of overhyped. It was simply the most erotic thing she had ever experienced in her twenty-nine years on earth.

His tongue was sublime velvet. His lips were nectar of the gods. But what really rocked her world were the feelings he evoked in her.

She heard a humming deep inside her, and an electric tingling raced through every nerve ending. Her nipples tightened. Her skin burned. Her sex dripped for him.

"Julie," he whispered against her mouth, "you taste so damned good."

Did he feel it, too? This wild rush of chemical reaction?

His hand slid up underneath the back of her T-shirt. He pulled her closer. His erection was iron against her thigh. Oh, yeah, he felt it, too.

Her body burned wherever his mouth touched—her cheek, her chin, her forehead, her eyelids.

Sleeping with a guy you'd just met was risky behavior, she knew that, but oddly enough she felt safe with Sebastian and she had to trust her feelings. She knew what she wanted and her gut was telling her she wasn't wrong about him.

Blindly, without purposeful thought, Julie lightly ran her tongue along the pounding pulse at the juncture of his throat and collarbone. He tasted salty. His rugged skin tightened beneath her mouth and a rough groan escaped his lips.

The pressure inside her was so intense she couldn't stand it a minute longer. Julie tugged at his pressed dress shirt, popping off a few buttons in her hurry to get him naked. He wore a white T-shirt underneath and he didn't protest when she grabbed it in her fists and tore it off his body.

The ripping sound was so satisfying. Good girls didn't recklessly rip up clothing. She liked being a bad girl.

"Hey, babe, slow down," Sebastian cooed. "You've got nothing to prove."

"I want you inside of me," she growled. "And I'm tired of waiting."

His eyes darkened, glittered wetly with a challenge. "You want it hard and fast?"

"Yes," Julie demanded and then nipped his bottom lip up between her teeth.

Her declaration inspired him. He raised her up with his arms, pinned her against the wall, spearing his knee roughly between her legs. Goaded by her, abandoning all restraint, he lowered his head and took her mouth like a hostile invader taking over a country.

Savagely, he plundered her mouth until she was breathless and quivering. "This the way you want it?"

"Yes," she declared again through gritted teeth. "Give it to me hard."

She had to have him inside her or go mad. She didn't know where this sexual aggression was coming from. It wasn't like her. But that was good. Healthy.

The old Julie had been too meek, too mild, too romantic by half. She embraced her passion. Let go of her inhibitions and submerged herself in sensation.

He ripped off her shirt the way she'd ripped off his, exposing her black lace bra underneath. Sebastian flicked his tongue all along the edge of the skimpy material and then suckled her nipples through the lace.

Julie burned.

Moaned.

She ran her hands down the length of his bare back, slipped her palms past the waistband of his pants, cupping his hard, tight buttocks. So nice!

Using his teeth, he pulled her bra down, leaving it tangled, almost immobilizing her arms.

Gently, oh, so gently, he bit one of her nipples. His sharp teeth against her tender skin made her gasp in surprise, but it didn't hurt. In fact, what she felt was the exact opposite of pain. It was physical pleasure of the highest order.

He loosened his grip on her, letting her slide down the wall while he did dizzy things to her with his tongue. Julie went for the button and then the zipper of his trousers, fumbling in the process, but finally managing to get his pants down.

Sebastian was eager to help. He gripped her buttocks, tightly pushing her up to meet his penis straining against his navy blue silk boxer briefs.

"Get 'em off," she muttered, and in a second he was fully exposed for her to feast her eyes upon.

Julie sucked in her breath at the glorious sight of the naked man. He was just as fine as she'd imagined he would be.

"Screw me," she said fiercely, amazing and thrilling herself with her brazenness.

"Get the condom out of my pants pocket," he said. "And roll it on me."

"You brought a condom with you?"

"You bet I did. Whenever I'm around you I can't keep my hands to myself."

For some reason, that thrilled her. She retrieved the condom from the pocket of his slacks, tore the packet with her teeth and then dropped to her knees to roll the condom on him.

"Come here." He reached down to her, pulled her up off her knees and shucked down her pants. Then he thrust into her hard and quick and took her breath away. But she was so dripping wet for him he slid right in as if he'd always belonged there.

The air smelled of their lust. He made a hissing sound of absolute pleasure. "You feel so good, babe. So tight and warm."

They made love like feral animals. Scratching and grappling. Banging against the walls. Arching their bodies—slippery with sweat—into each other.

Wildly giving vent to heated moans and deep-throat yelps, their mating was feverish and mindlessly, purely elemental. Julie wrapped her legs tight around Sebastian's waist. He held her with her back pressed against the wall, slamming into her.

"Harder," she begged.

He complied, pounding her until her sex throbbed with the sweetest ache in the entire world.

"More, give me more." She wanted him as deep inside her as he could get.

He silenced her with a kiss, but his thrusts became even more fervent as he plunged deeper and deeper until she feared his big, hard cock would rip her right in two.

Sebastian plowed one hand up the back of her neck, threading his thick fingers through her hair. He pulled her head back, exposing her throat. He suckled on her skin, moving kisses down toward her breasts again.

She reached down to caress the shaft of his penis as it slipped in and out of her. She brought up her fingers, dripping with her own juices, and smeared the wetness over her swollen breasts.

Sebastian opened his mouth wide over her nipple, taking in as much of her flesh as he could, suckling her as if he wanted to swallow her whole.

Julie gasped, almost sobbing with the exquisiteness of the sensation.

He groaned her name and then he just groaned. He kissed her hard, thrusting his tongue in her mouth as his cock thrust up hard inside of her.

She was close. So damned close.

His corded muscles tightened against her, his buttocks stiffened. He was close, too.

Blood pulsed hot and fast through her veins. Her womb clenched. She looked into his eyes and he looked into hers and time simply evaporated.

"You keep doing that and I'm gonna blow."

"Doing what?"

"Squeezing me like that."

"Like this?" She flexed her inner muscles.

He groaned. "Vixen."

She grinned.

"Please don't make me come yet. I want you to go first," he said, slowing his rhythm. "What's it going to take?"

She touched the tip of her tongue to her upper lip. "You're doing it."

"Come for me, sweetheart," he crooned, his voice low and guttural. "I want to see your face when you come."

Sebastian moved faster then and deeper than she ever thought possible.

In an instant, Julie felt sensations splintering inside her. Orgasm clutched her. She moaned out his name and all the air left her body as explosion after explosion rolled through her body.

"Julie," Sebastian whispered. "Jules."

He shoved into her one last plunging thrust and she felt the convulsive throb of his release let loose.

"Jules," he whispered again. "Bright as diamonds." He buried his face against her neck and held her tight.

Slowly, in a tangle of hazy lust and sweaty limbs, they sank to the floor.

LIMP AND SATED, Julie lay snuggled in Sebastian's arms. The man had not disappointed. The thought of all the other delicious things they could do together made her shiver.

Sebastian shifted her closer to him, spooning against her with his strong male body. She thrilled to the warmth and size of him. He was large enough to take care of her. It was not a progressive, modern thought, but the primal woman in her couldn't help thinking it.

He held her loosely. Letting her know he was there, but she could easily pull away if she wanted.

She didn't want to pull away.

He kissed her temple.

This felt so nice. Almost as good as the sex. She could stay like this for the rest of her life.

Whoa! Don't get attached. It's just sex.

It sounded good. It was what she wanted, but even as she

struggled to concentrate on nothing but his physical attributes and how sensually their bodies joined, she couldn't help hoping for something more.

Stop the fanciful thinking.

There couldn't be anything more between them *because...*

His distracting fingertips reached up to feather her hair back off her forehead. His fingers caressing her temple felt so good she almost forgot what she'd been thinking about.

Oh, yeah, she couldn't allow there to be anything more than sex between them because every time she made love with a guy she fell *in* love with him and invariably got her heart broken. This time, things were going to be different. This time, she was going to live in the here and now and just enjoy the ride. No expectations, no guilt, no Cinderella dreams or castles in the sky.

But deep down inside, she knew Sebastian was different from either Phillip or Roger.

You can't let that influence you.

What did she want from him?

Sex. That was it. Sex and the ability to switch off her emotions from her body.

"I'd like to do that again," Sebastian murmured, his warm breath tickling her ear.

"Now?" Julie didn't know if she was up for another round like that one. Not this quick.

"Now, later, whatever I can get. I'm jonesing for you, babe."

She shifted in his arms so she could see his face. His eyes were sultry, his lids half-lowered. Her heart bumped into her chest. "You're not getting addicted to me, are you?"

He looked surprised. "Are you getting addicted to me?"

"I don't even like you, why would I get addicted to you?"

Julie nudged him to show she was kidding, and he nudged her back, apparently getting it. Like it or not, the man was tuned in to her frequency.

"Do you even like me?" He cracked a smile.

"No."

"Aw, come on. Why not? I'm fun and I know how to have a good time."

"You're also arrogant, conceited, high-handed, egotistical—"

"Don't forget vainglorious," he teased.

She tangled her fingers in the tuft of dark hairs at his chest. "You're never going to let me live that down, are you?"

"Nope." His eyes were languid and tender and calm and she allowed herself to loiter in them. She reached and swept a finger across the tips of his midnight-black lashes, drew it down the angle of his nose and then landed on his mouth and traced the angular outline.

He shifted and for the first time, she saw the tattoo on his shoulder. It was small, about the size of a quarter, done in blue ink. An eagle in flight. She pressed her lips against it. "What's this?"

"Youthful indiscretion," he said.

"Were you in the military?"

He shrugged. "Nope."

"Why the eagle?"

"It symbolizes freedom."

"Free as a bird?"

"Something like that."

A calm settled over her. *I have chosen the right lover. He's not going to get attached.*

"It's good," she said.

"Good?"

"That you value freedom."

"I suppose."

She propped herself up on one elbow. "Why?"

"WHY WHAT?" Sebastian asked.

"Why is freedom so important to you?"

"I guess I hate the thought of missing out on something." Sebastian pushed the tip of her nose with an index finger. He loved lying here looking at her. Her eyes were so earnest. He laid an arm around her waist, savoring the feel of her soft, silky skin. He was so glad he'd come here tonight, even if she was peppering him with questions. "Probably because I missed out on so much when I was a kid."

"Like what?" She snuggled closer to him. "What did you miss out on?"

"Having a father, for one thing."

"You never knew your dad?"

"I knew who he was. He was a son of a bitch."

"I'm sorry."

"Hey, it wasn't your fault."

"What did he do?"

He toyed with a strand of her hair. He didn't like talking about his old man. "Ever heard of Simon Black?"

"The lead singer for the British rock band Bruise?"

She sounded impressed. Women always sounded impressed when they found out about his father. Sebastian didn't know why. There was nothing to be impressed about. The man was an abusive alcoholic with far more money than humanity.

"That'd be him."

"Wow, what was it like growing up with a rock-star dad?"

"I didn't grow up with him. My mother was a groupie. He got her pregnant, told her to have an abortion and trotted off on a world tour. She decided to keep me. She tried to get him to have a relationship with me. He came around a time or two. Christmas. My sixth birthday. I never saw him after Mom died and Aunt Bunnie came to get me and Linc and took us off to live at the commune."

She sucked in her breath. Sympathy swam in her eyes. She reached out to rub his upper arm.

"Don't go feeling sorry for me." He hardened his chin. "I did just fine without him."

"How did you cope?"

"Threw myself into life. I made lots of friends in spite of my shabby wardrobe. I was class president, prom king, the captain of the debate team and I batted cleanup on my high school baseball squad. My advanced placement classes started at seven a.m. and after-school activities kept me busy until nine at night. No time to feel sorry for myself."

"Oh, you were *that* guy," she teased.

"Which girl were you?"

"The shy one hiding out in the library reading *Romeo and Juliet* and dreaming of dating the class president, prom king, debate-team captain, baseball hero."

He grinned at her. "So you were *that* girl."

"Yep, the one you didn't give a second glance."

"Forgive me, that was damned rude of me."

"You're forgiven."

He was tired of talking about himself. He wanted to find out more about her. "How about you? What do you value, Julie DeMarco?"

She hesitated a moment. "I'm not sure anymore."

"Why not?"

"My life's in flux. I'm in the process of reevaluating my values."

"Is that so."

"You know, I think I might like to give that freedom thing a try. You make is sound so fun."

"Kind of hard for a caretaker type."

"What do you mean?"

"It's hard to fly free when your basic orientation is to help people. Look how emotionally invested you got over Colin Cruz," Sebastian pointed out.

"What's so wrong about caring?"

"Nothing's wrong with it. It's just that it's hard to care too deeply and still fly free."

"You're saying you don't care about anything?"

"No, I'm saying freedom is more important to me than other things." He laced his fingers through hers. It felt nice, this bonding. "Thing is, you have to make choices in life. No matter what the media would have us believe, you can't really have it all. You make one choice, you close yourself off to all the other opportunities out there. When you fly free, you don't close off your options."

"But neither do you get the intimacy of being deeply involved."

"That's true."

"Choices," she said, and a pensive look came into her eyes.

"Julie," he murmured, squeezing her fingers tighter. "You think too much."

"How do you know I'm thinking?"

He pressed the pad of his thumb between her eyebrows. "You get the cutest furrow right here when your mind is clicking on high gear."

"I hate that I'm so easy to read."

"Don't. It's endearing."

"It gets me into hot water is what it does."

"What kind of hot water?"

"In the past, I've been rather foolish in love. I wear my heart on my sleeve."

"Ah," he said, hating the fact she'd been hurt. She deserved to be cherished.

By who? You? That's a laugh. You've never had a relationship that outlived the expiration date on your milk cartoon.

"'Ah'?" she prompted.

"That explains it."

"Explains what?"

"The insistence on just sex, no dating."

"Yeah." Her voice lowered, thickened. She blinked, cleared her throat. "From now on I've got a Teflon heart."

"Sounds smart."

"It is."

He kissed her. Softly. Sweetly.

She made encouraging noises.

Slowly, he tasted her and then he gently increased the pressure, but kept things light and playful, realizing this was exactly what they both needed right now. He was really getting into the kiss when she pulled away.

"I get why women are so crazy about you," she said. "And it's not just the looks. You're great at making a woman feel special. What I don't get is why no one has snared you."

"It's that freedom thing. I don't stay in one place too long. Gotta keep moving." He nibbled her earlobe.

"Always on the run."

He didn't run from things. He ran to them. New jobs, new adventures, new women. Except suddenly, he didn't want any more women. He wanted only Julie.

The realization was startling and it twisted him up inside.

"I like that about you," she whispered. "I know I don't have to worry about you getting serious on me. You're foot-loose and fancy-free and you don't let anything stand in your way."

"That's me," he said, surprised that his voice came out husky and hollow. "Footloose and fancy-free."

She kissed his chin, then moved her lips down his jaw to his throat. Wherever her lips touched, his body burst into tiny flames. And she was doing wondrous things to him with her tongue.

He couldn't believe he was so hot and ready for her again this soon. She seemed to have an unerring talent for knowing just how to excite his libido.

But despite the urgency holding him in a vise grip, this time he wanted something slow and tender. He wrapped his thighs around her waist, flipped her onto her back and positioned himself above her, pinning her wrists to the floor.

He pressed his forehead to hers and stared deeply into her gentle blue eyes. She looked like peace. Calm and serene. He supported his weight on his forearms. His cock was throbbing steel between their pelvises. Her soft breasts were pressed flushed against his hard chest.

Her breathing was his air. The thump of her heart vibrated through him, infused him.

Without ever taking his eyes off her, he slowly entered her body. She made a soft, happy sound. He felt something hot and sticky deep inside his chest.

Driven by a force he could not explain, Sebastian stopped moving. He cupped her cheek with his palm and looked at her. Really truly looked at her and in that strange and incredible moment he felt he was being given a glimpse of his future if he only had the courage to wrap his hand around it and seize it before it slipped away.

The emotion bloomed, growing into something he dared not name, but had spent his entire life avoiding. It was an emotion cloaked by fear. He was that little boy again, afraid to love, afraid to invest himself, determined not to get hurt.

The feeling clogged his throat, crowded his chest, tightened his lungs. This kind of sensation did not fit in to his plans. Just the inkling of it stifled his freedom.

All at once he had a desperate urge to run. Just get up and take off buck-naked out the door. He'd never planned for this feeling and he had no idea what to do about it.

It was at that precise moment Sebastian Black knew he was in serious trouble.

DAMMIT, THE SABOTEUR'S plan to bring more scandal down on Confidential Rejuvenations hadn't worked. Installing a camera in the therapy room and broadcasting a live video stream of Colin Cruz's dirty sex-addict confessions had backfired.

And all because of that interfering Sebastian Black.

He, Colin Cruz and Confidential Rejuvenations had all come out smelling like roses.

Now there had to be a new scandal. Something Black couldn't spin his way out of. Something juicy and salacious.

Sebastian Black needed to be caught with his pants down and the saboteur knew exactly how to do it and which paparazzo to call....

10

SEBASTIAN WOKE UP on Julie's floor. He had a crick in his neck and two more in his back.

And he'd never felt so good.

He stretched, then looked around for Julie.

She wasn't there.

"Jules?" he called, getting to his feet and searching for his clothes. When she didn't answer, he headed in the direction of where he supposed her bedroom was. He rapped on the door. "Julie?"

No answer.

He turned the knob and pushed the door open, thinking maybe she'd let him take her to breakfast, only to discover her canopied bed was made up. The room was definitely Julie, decorated in pinks and floral prints and lots of lace. Wistfulness washed over him and he had no idea why. Quickly, he backed out and shut the door.

"Julie?" He searched the entire apartment, but she was no where to be found.

Then, he discovered the note on the kitchen counter.

Thanks for a great time. I'm off to yoga class with Vanessa. Let yourself out.—J.

Apparently all he rated was a hastily scribbled note. No good-morning wake-up kiss. No cuddling. No showering together. No sharing breakfast. Sebastian snorted, wadded up the note and tossed it in the trash can.

Hell, you'd think she could have at least roused him for a cup of coffee instead of leaving him lying naked and alone on her living room carpet. In the past, he would have admired a woman who took lovemaking so casually, but today, he was feeling…

Used.

Sebastian didn't like the feeling, nor did he understand it. He was the one who'd come over here. He was the one who'd put the moves on Julie and now he was the one acting like a pouty kid who hadn't gotten his way. What was up with that?

The happy mood he'd woken up with vanished. He dressed and drove back to his hotel to shower and change before heading over to Confidential Rejuvenations to deal with the aftermath of the Colin Cruz incident.

He ended up in the temporary office Dr. Butler had assigned to him, glowering down at the spreadsheets he'd assembled over the past several days. His initial thought had been to cross-reference the incidents of sabotage with the days the employees, the hospital co-owners and the board members had been on the premises.

Starting back in the early spring, there'd been a tabloid leak to the paparazzi about a beleaguered pop star undergoing treatment for drug and alcohol abuse, a kitchen fire attributed to arson, several small-scale thefts, a transformer knocked out and the backup generator tampered with, car tires slashed in the employee parking lot and this last mess with the camera in the group therapy room.

The spreadsheets were telling him only five people had

been on the hospital campus on the day of every single one of those incidents. Maxine Woodbury, Carlisle Jones, Devi Parker, Roger Marshall and Julie DeMarco.

Seeing Roger's and Julie's names on the list caused his gut to squeeze. He simply could not believe Julie was involved, but Roger? He didn't know the man.

Sebastian blew out his breath and splayed a palm against the back of his neck, considering the consequences of Roger being the culprit. That'd go over big with Linc if he were the one to blow the whistle on Keeley's father. But why would a man of Roger's stature and prestige stoop to something as petty and cowardly as sabotage?

Then again, why would anyone on the list do such a thing? Maxine was a sixty-nine-year-old grandmother. Carlisle Jones had a wife and kids to support. Devi Parker was a professional businesswoman. And Julie…well she was just too nice to pull something like this.

You act is if you know her. Just because you've slept with her doesn't mean you know her.

He shook his head. No. He refused to even entertain the thought that Julie was somehow involved. Besides, it might not be any of those five. It could be a contract worker or a patient. He shouldn't jump to conclusions.

Knuckles rapped against his open door. Sebastian looked up to see Tanner standing there.

"May I talk to you?"

"Sure." Sebastian motioned him inside. "What's up?"

Tanner shut the door behind him and walked over to sink into the chair beside the desk. "I'm ready to put a stop to this damned sabotage. Butler, Covey and Garcia don't want the police involved, but I don't think the perpetrator is just going to stop."

"I agree."

"The saboteur knows this hospital inside and out. When the tires were slashed in the employee parking lot, we didn't catch who'd done it because the security cameras had been disabled. I'm certain it's an inside job."

Sebastian studied Tanner a long moment. "Why are you bringing this to me?"

"I need someone to help me that I know for sure isn't involved. Someone sharp and savvy that I can count on. I've cross-referenced the employees who were at the hospital on the day that all the incidents of sabotage occurred. Of course, in the case of the Web camera, it could have been in there for days and no one knew about it until the live stream last night and that could have been triggered remotely via any computer."

Sebastian sucked in his breath. "I cross-referenced my own list."

Tanner's eyes darkened. "So you know Julie's name is on it."

"I do."

Their gazes met.

"You saved our ass on this Colin Cruz thing. I've gotta tell you I'm damned embarrassed it happened on my watch. I won't allow anything like that to happen again," Tanner continued.

"No clues on who installed the camera in the session room?"

"We dusted the camera, the painting and the wall for fingerprints but we only found Colin's prints. Either the culprit wore gloves or wiped everything down after the camera was installed, or both. The thing is we never know when this person or persons will strike again or what they'll do."

"You think it could be more than one person?"

Tanner shrugged. "I'm considering all possibilities."

"Carlisle seems the most likely to me," Sebastian said. "As head of the maintenance department he's got access to the entire hospital, plus he has the knowledge and skill to do things like dismantle your security cameras."

"It's not Carlisle. He's a good friend and an honest man."

"Are you certain it couldn't be him?"

"As certain as anyone can be. He has absolutely no motive."

Sebastian got to his feet. "Well, it sure as hell isn't Julie."

"Of course not," Tanner said, also standing up. "She has no motive, either."

"So that leaves Maxine Woodbury, Devi Parker and Roger Marshall."

"Our chief suspects are a little old lady, a sex therapist and Dr. Butler's best golfing buddy. All with no motives."

"It was pretty suspicious that Devi Parker was late the same day Colin Cruz has a meltdown and she told Julie to start the session without her."

"Yes but..." Tanner shook his head. "Devi? That's hard to swallow. It could still be someone else. Maybe someone slipped into the hospital on their day off and we have no record of them being on the grounds."

"That's true. What's your plan?"

"I could cross-reference the spreadsheet with the guard logs. Every car that comes in or goes out is recorded. That would widen the suspect list." Tanner rested his hands on his hips. "I was also thinking of installing special surveillance cameras. Tiny, discreet, waterproof. I'd put them up in strategic locations and monitor them myself on my laptop. No need to involve my security team."

"Spy cameras?"

"Yes. And only you and I would know about them."

"Depending on where you put these cameras, you could run into privacy issues."

"It's a risk I'm willing to take."

"I'll back you up."

Tanner reached out to shake his hand. "Let's catch us a saboteur."

THE PLAN WAS IN MOTION.

Soon, very soon, Sebastian Black and Julie DeMarco were going to take a very big fall.

The saboteur laughed and put the name of a publicity-hungry paparazzo on speed dial.

DR. BUTLER, Dr. Covey and Robert Garcia took Sebastian out to dinner to thank him for adroitly handling the Colin Cruz episode.

"It could have been a fiasco," Dr. Covey said as they lingered over brandy and cigars at one of the most expensive steak restaurants in Austin.

"You were amazing," Dr. Butler enthused. "You're worth every penny we're paying you."

Normally, he would have done a bit of grandstanding and reveled in his success, but tonight he was feeling edgy and impatient and he couldn't wait to call Julie. He hadn't seen her all day and he was anxious to get together with her again.

"Mr. Black?"

Sebastian turned, saw a waiter standing at his elbow, a silver tray balanced on his upturned palm. "Yes?"

The man extended the tray.

He spied the envelope with his name on it. What was this about? He took the envelope, tipped the waiter, then excused himself from the group. He slipped into the empty hallway, opened the envelope and read the cryptic typewritten message that made him smile.

> Meet me in the Confidential Rejuvenations' meditation room in the tranquility garden at eleven-fifteen. Be naked.

JULIE HAD SPENT the day alternating between overanalyzing what had happened with Sebastian and trying not to think about it. She was so confused. Part of her kept hoping he'd show up on the floor to talk to her, while another part of her was hoping he didn't show. She didn't know if she could look into his snapping black eyes and not fall madly in love with him.

Almost her entire shift had passed and nothing. No sign of him. Nor had he called her. She told herself that was a good thing, but it didn't stop her body from getting raw and achy. Everything seemed arousing. The way the material of her scrub suit rubbed across her breasts when she moved. The smell of the floral boutique centerpiece on the nurses' station. The soft sound of the evocative mood music piped through the hospital's sound system.

Toward the end of the evening, she reached into her pocket for the key to lock up the medication room and her fingers brushed against a small white envelope.

What was this? How had it gotten into her pocket?

Heart jackhammering, she looked around to see if anyone had noticed her. The only staff member in view was the ward secretary, Maxine, and she was busy tapping on the keyboard at her computer terminal.

The night-shift nurses were arriving, putting their things

away, chatting to each other. Julie slipped past them, headed for the locker room. She went into an empty bathroom stall and shut the door.

Pulse pounding, she unfolded the typewritten note.

> Meet me in the meditation room of the tranquility gardens at eleven twenty-five. Be prepared for the thrill of your life.

AT ELEVEN-TWENTY, Sebastian paced naked inside the enclosure of the meditation room of the Confidential Rejuvenations' tranquility garden.

Another few minutes passed.

Just when Sebastian was about to put his clothes back on and go in search of her, he heard footsteps on the walkway.

Pulse galloping, he held his breath, stepped to the back of the meditation room, away from the window. His breath came in short gasps. Sweat slicked his body. The throbbing between his thighs intensified.

Every muscle in his body tensed. He waited, awash in sensation.

Silence.

Another minute passed and then another. Where was she?

He edged to the door, cracked it open, peered out into the garden.

No one. Nothing.

He looked down at the walkway and spied a candle, a lighter and another note right outside the door.

He snatched up the candle, lighter and note and brought them back inside the meditation room. He lit the candle, read the note.

Turn on the surround sound system.

He punched Play on the CD player, soothing music whispered through the speakers.

Uneasiness mixed with expectancy rippled inside of him and sent his arousal shooting through the roof. She'd stripped him bare, left him vulnerable, at her mercy, but dammit, it made him want her even more.

Just what wicked game was she playing?

CONFIDENTIAL Rejuvenations' new meditation sanctuary was nestled inside the tranquility gardens overlooking the banks of the Colorado River. During the day, acupuncture, massage and other alternative healing practices were offered there. But after dark, the meditation room was kept locked.

How had Sebastian finagled a key?

You have to ask? The man could charm the skin off a snake.

Julie walked down the path, self-consciousness mingling with curiosity, desire and a heightened awareness of her surroundings. She felt deliciously wanton.

Heat radiated from her feminine core throughout her entire body. She'd darted out the back entrance of the hospital, knowing the security cameras were on her, watching her. It only served to escalate her arousal. She forced herself to keep moving. She was doing nothing wrong by taking a walk in the moonlight.

The air was chilly and she was grateful for her jacket. The full moon reflected ghostly white off the flagstone walkway. The farther down the path she went, the more her knees quivered.

What was she going to find in the meditation sanctuary?

The grounds were eerie at night. Julie took a deep breath to bolster her courage as she neared the gardens, which were tucked away behind a copse of pecan trees just off the flagstone walkway.

She stepped out of the moonlight and into the shadows. The breeze picked up, shook the trees, knocked loose pecans. They hit the ground with ominous plopping noises. Julie gulped and knocked at the door of the meditation sanctuary.

It creaked open on its hinges.

Inside, the building was pitch-black and smelled of the fragrant hyacinth and lavender incense used to relax guests. She heard the soft tinkling of wind chimes and realized it was the sound track to new age music playing softly in the background.

"Hello?" she murmured and tentatively stepped across the threshold. "Anyone here?"

From one of the rooms in the back, she caught a flicker of light. A candle?

She inched forward. "Sebastian?"

Goose bumps popped up on her arms.

He appeared in the doorway, the candle in his hand. The sight of him left her breathless. He was totally and completely naked. His eyes glittered like black diamonds.

Then he grinned that sexy big-bad-wolf grin of his and Julie's heart swelled with a fresh tumble of emotions.

"Shut the door," he said in that deep voice that stirred her on so many levels. "And lock it behind you."

Helpless to resist, she did as he asked.

"Follow me." He turned and disappeared into the darkness.

The bobbing candle lit her way. She followed him into

the meditation room. One entire wall was made of slate and a curtain of water trickled down it in a gentle cascade.

In the middle of the room lay a massage table, covered with a beige flannel sheet. The music came from this room. Low chiming gongs vibrated all around her.

He set the candle on the stone counter that held an assortment of interesting-looking oils and lotions and then turned back to her.

She took two steps away, felt her eyes widening with nervousness anticipation.

The devilish expression on Sebastian's face held a pledge of pure sin, and Julie experienced a blast of sensation that squeezed her womb and tensed her clit. Her mind was so fogged with desire she couldn't think straight. Could do nothing, in fact, but peer into his mesmerizing gaze.

Sebastian patted the massage chair. "Sit up here."

She felt like Eve being offered that first deadly apple and she was compelled.

He reached out a hand to touch her and she was amazed to discover a simple brushing of his fingertips could trigger such an overwhelming awareness inside her. He lowered his eyelashes and her body responded.

"Come," he said.

She went.

It was as if something were settling into place. She felt a click. As if a lid and a jar had come together.

But she saw it in his eyes, too. She wasn't the only one feeling this connection.

You're romanticizing him. Stop it. Remember, this is about sex and nothing else.

Right. She was leaving her heart out of the equation. The

pulse at the hollow of her throat throbbed. "You're going to torture me with pleasure, aren't you?"

"Mmm."

His muscular body was so amazing she couldn't stop looking at it.

Julie narrowed her eyes. The candlelight bathed him in a muted orange glow and dark shadows. His insouciant playboy stare belied the steadfastness of his powerful chin, the trustworthy promise of his chiseled cheekbones.

For the first time, she saw the contradictions in him. He wasn't as footloose and unfettered as he wanted people to believe. There was more to him than the glossy surface, even as he struggled to keep people from seeing it. He courted his reputation as a swinging bachelor. But an image was all that it was. She wondered if there was a scrap of truth beneath the facade.

She found the contrast between his features and his lifestyle striking. He wasn't as slick and smooth and superficial as he wanted everyone to believe. He was a country boy in rich clothing. A decent guy who'd sold out for the big bucks. A man who didn't believe his own hype, but had no idea what to replace it with.

An odd sadness curled inside her, pushing aside the excitement. Who was he really, this mysterious Mr. Sebastian Black?

The expression in his eyes went totally predatory as he held up his silk tie.

"What…" She could scarcely push the words past her throat. "What are you going to do with that?"

He stepped toward her. "Blindfold you."

She wasn't sure she liked this idea, but he gave her no time to resist. He wrapped the tie around her head. The thick hairs at his wrist grazed the side of her temple and she felt his muscles flex. He was so powerful. She was completely at his mercy here; hidden away from everyone.

And, yet, she trusted him implicitly.

Slowly, he undressed her. She didn't speak. She didn't want to do anything that would make him stop.

Nimbly, his fingers eased off her scrub pants. His nails felt smooth, but beyond that she was aware of faint but rough calluses on his fingertips.

Old scars.

The farm boy underneath the spin-doctor gloss.

She felt the air against her skin as he stripped her naked. She could hear his breathing, harsh and ragged. She wished she could see his face.

His lips brushed hers, soft and light as butterfly wings. He kissed her.

She inhaled, filling her lungs with his languid heat.

He broke off the kiss. "Lay down." He used his hand to guide her up onto the massage table. The flannel sheet was soft against her skin.

"I need to feel you," she whispered.

"Spread your legs."

She spread her legs. Sensation rippled inside her. He grasped her by the hips, scooted her to the edge of the table and then positioned himself between her legs. His bare skin rubbed against her sensitive inner thighs. She could feel his erection growing harder.

"Feel me now?" he growled.

"I want to feel your face." Like a blind woman, she reached up to his jaw and traced the fresh sprout of beard stubble.

Slowly, she ran her fingertips up both sides of his face, skimmed his cheekbones, his nose, his eyelids. Here the skin was soft, in sharp contrast to the rest of him. With her index finger, she etched his eyebrows, delighting in their bristly thickness. It astounded her, how much more aware she was of him now that she could not see him.

He leaned down, used a finger to push the hair back from her right ear and then he wet the outer edge with his tongue.

The sensation was exquisite.

He blew across her damp skin. She gasped. Then when he took her earlobe between his teeth and nibbled, she moaned softly.

She loved the game he was playing. Secretly, she'd dream of a lover who'd play such erotic games with her. A man who understood the power of the imagination. He was teaching her all kinds of interesting things about herself.

Oddly, it felt as if she'd known him forever.

"Roll over on your stomach."

She shifted onto her belly and felt a tumbling sensation inside her. The room was thick with the smell of hyacinth and lavender and candle wax and her juicy sex. She was so wet for him.

Julie heard him move away from the table. Heard bottles clinking and she was tempted to lift up the corner of the blindfold to see what was going on, but just as she raised her hand, he clicked his tongue. "No peeking."

"What are you up to?"

"Shh."

Her body tensed. The waiting was killing her.

The heated oil hit the small of her back in a slow drizzle, the unexpectedness of it forcing the air from her body.

Then came his hands, thick and strong. Kneading her soft, vulnerable flesh.

"Oh, my…" She sighed.

The way he was caressing her made her feel as if she was the most cherished woman in the world. His touch pushed a fever of sexual desire up her spine to the base of her brain.

Amidst the scent of oil and candle and her own femininity, she caught a whiff of his scent. He smelled of the autumn woods, earthy and real.

He rubbed her back and just as she was settling into the rhythmic motion, he changed the game by leaning down and firmly, but lightly, biting her butt.

Julie squealed at the erotic sensations shooting through her, and raised her head up off the massage table.

"Too hard?" he asked earnestly.

"Just right. Perfect. Almost too perfect. How is it you know exactly what to do at exactly the right moment?"

His response was a self-satisfied chuckle.

Which sort of pissed her off. She didn't like that he knew her body so well when he barely knew her. Was she that easy to read?

"On your back," he said.

She hesitated, but finally, because she wanted so much more from him, she did as he asked.

Once she was over, he kissed her again. As sweetly as before, as if sensing she needed calming. His lips soothed her jangled nerves and banished any lingering irritation she might be feeling.

For what felt like hours—maybe it was, she'd lost all sense of time—he kissed her most feminine lips, sliding his pagan tongue in and out of her aching moistness. The external world fell away and it was just the two of them inside this sweltering cocoon of pure, primal sex. The only noise in the room was the soft meditation music and the slippery wet sounds his greedy mouth was making against her hungry flesh.

He used his fingers to hold her lips wide open as he lashed her with that tongue. In and out. In and out. Driving her blindly mad.

It was torture. She wanted to come so badly, but he wasn't allowing it. Wanting, needing to fall over the cliff, but hanging poised on the edge of it.

She moaned his name.

"Yes, Julie," he croaked. It sounded as if his mouth was as dry as hers.

"I want you inside me."

"No," he said. "Not yet." Then he went back to his task, probing her more deeply than before.

She cried out as his tongue found her center. She was drunk with it. With his mouth. With him.

His tongue was an exquisite instrument of torture. His fingers a tool of sweet torment.

"I can't take it anymore," she said. "I want to ride you."

She ripped off the tie, flung it to the floor, got to her feet.

Sebastian swallowed hard, glorying in the sight of her standing before him beautiful and naked.

"Your turn to lie down," she ordered.

He lay on the massage table and she straddled him. Lowering her head and kissing him, her hair formed a sexy curtain around them, and her mouth swallowed him up as if she could read his mind and knew every aberrant thought crossing it.

She ran her fingernails over his rock-hard flesh.

"Ride me," he growled.

"I thought you'd never ask."

She slowly eased herself down on the length of him. His

hands went up to span her waist, holding her in place. He let out his breath on a long, controlled exhale. Her wetness engulfed him. A feminine sea. He was inside her.

She rocked above him, hard and fast, her face twisted in concentration. She looked so gorgeous, making love to him. She pushed him deeper and deeper into the padded table. She rode him hard.

Sebastian flew. Soaring high. He'd never felt so free.

The union was quick and hurried, frantic and feverish. They galloped together.

Everything was wide open. They fused and flowed into each other. It felt so right. So perfect. The sensations were maddeningly complicated. Sebastian couldn't distinguish where he ended and she began. They were two together. One no more.

He was beyond thinking. Beyond awareness. He was nothing but a hard throbbing cock embedded in her sweetness.

Relentlessly, Julie made love to him. Sliding up, coming down hard. Again and again. He arched his back, thrust his pelvis. He had to stuff his fist against his mouth to stay the primal cry.

He was gonna blow.

"Julie," he gasped past his own fist.

And then, he lost it.

Twitching and jerking, Sebastian shot into her. He could not breathe. He'd never experienced an orgasm this strong. It was all over him, around him, in him. He could taste it. Taste her. It was cinnamon and lust and…something else he could not name.

His cock started to get hard all over again.

The things she was making him feel were damned unsettling. He couldn't stop thinking about her. Or wanting her.

And not just in his bed. He wanted her on his arm. He wanted to show her off. He wanted to tell everyone they were dating.

He'd lost control and in all his thirty years on earth he'd never lost control because of a woman. It bothered him. This power she wielded. Not just over his libido.

But over his heart.

11

JULIE FELT HAPPIER than she'd ever felt in her life. She propped herself up on one elbow and lay watching Sebastian sleep, her eyes tracing the outlines of his handsome face in the light from the flickering candle.

He'd spoiled her for good. After him, no other man could ever compare.

She was so lucky to have met him, to know him. His gentle touch, debonair smile and sexy wink opened the door to a whole new world of sensation and she would be forever grateful. He'd given her back the self-esteem Roger had stolen away. Sebastian had been the perfect teacher. She his willing student.

But soon he would be headed back for California. She was going to miss him.

Sadness stabbed her chest and she bit down on her bottom lip. She didn't want him to go, but she knew this was the most critical stage of their affair. The moment just before the breakup. It was okay. She'd managed to keep her heart out of the fray.

Did you? Did you really?

She looked over at him and her breath caught in her lungs. She hadn't fallen in love with him. Yes, they had a good time. Yes, they had chemistry. And yes, if he stayed much longer, she probably would fall in love with him. He was a hard man not to love.

Just because she'd been thinking about him pretty well nonstop since the day he'd walked onto her floor, didn't mean she was in love with Sebastian. Obsessed with his body, maybe, but she wasn't in love.

She'd gone into this relationship knowing nothing could come of it. That was okay. He'd taught her so much. And she understood exactly what it was that she *did* want. She wanted a man who wanted her with a passion that burned so brightly he couldn't notice any other woman. She wanted a man who would give up everything to be with her. And she knew that was not Sebastian Black.

Julie refused to second-guess herself. She had grown and changed. She'd learned so much about her own sexuality. A bright future beckoned.

A future without Sebastian.

An emotion she couldn't name twisted deep inside her chest, but she shoved aside the sensation, exhaled, clenched her fists.

You're just going to miss the great sex. That's all it is. It's nothing more complex than that.

And yet, she couldn't help wanting more.

She was hungry for more kisses, more caresses, more hot sex. She wanted to keep having screaming orgasms with him. And she liked the way she felt curled up tight against his naked body.

Let him go.

Dammit. She wasn't going to do this. She was *not* going to romanticize him. She wasn't going to ruin what had been a wonderful experience by foolishly hoping for more.

"It's over and you're going to be okay," she whispered and halfway convinced herself it was true.

"Did you say something?" he asked in a dozy voice.

She snuggled on top of him. "I said thank you for this little tryst. You're right. It's very thrilling. So tell me, just how did you get that note slipped into my pocket without me knowing it?"

"What do you mean?" He shifted, braced himself up on his elbows and raised up with Julie clinging to his chest. "I didn't put a note in your pocket. You're the one who sent me the note. By the way, how did you know I was at La Grange with Butler, Covey and Garcia?"

She sat up. "No, I didn't."

They stared at each other, wide-eyed.

"Well if you didn't send me a note at La Grange and I didn't put a note in your pocket telling me to meet you here, then who did?"

AT 6:00 A.M., the ringing telephone pulled Julie from a deep sleep. After her late-night rendezvous with Sebastian and the subsequent realization that someone other than themselves had set up the tryst, they'd hurriedly gotten dressed and he'd followed her to her apartment to make sure she got home okay. Then they'd both agreed it would be best for him to return to his hotel.

Julie grappled for the phone. "Hello," she mumbled.

"Have you seen the front page of this morning's edition of the *Inquisitive Tattler?*" Elle asked, referring to a daily Austin tabloid that preferred stories of scandal and gossip to legitimate reporting.

"No." The word came out on a whimper. She sat up and

flicked on the bedside lamp. And then she had to go and ask what she already knew in her heart. "What's on the cover?"

"You and Sebastian." Elle cleared her throat. "In…um… a rather compromising position."

"How compromising?"

"Julie, I want you to take a deep breath and—"

The phone beeped in Julie's ear. "Hang on, Elle. I've got another incoming call." She switch-hooked over to the new caller. "Hello."

"Jules, I knew you were looking to play the part of the bad girl, but I think you pushed the envelope just a little too far." It was Vanessa.

"You've seen the *Inquisitive Tattler.*"

"I didn't know Sebastian had a tattoo on his shoulder. What is that? An eagle?"

Julie groaned. Just how disastrous was this thing? "Hang on, I've got Elle on the other line."

"I'll let you go. I have surgery in an hour, but let's hook up later. Stay strong. 'Bye."

Nibbling her bottom lip, Julie wished she'd asked Sebastian to spend the night. Right now she needed his big strong arms around her in the worst way.

She switched over to Elle. "I'm back, it was Nessa."

The front doorbell rang.

"Listen, Elle, I gotta let you go. There's someone at the door."

"Remember, I'm here if you need me."

She hung up, slung back the covers, shuffled into her bathrobe and slippers and padded to the front door. She peeked through the peephole.

To see a reporter and a camera crew on her front porch.

Dear heavens, just what was on the front page of that tabloid?

The doorbell pealed again, but she didn't answer it. Instead, she slunk back to her bedroom, stuffed her legs into a pair of jeans and tugged a pink hooded sweatshirt over her head. She donned sneakers, slipped on a pair of dark sunglasses and stuck her wallet into her pocket.

The doorbell rang a third time.

Grateful for living in a first-floor apartment, she raised her bedroom window, yanked off the screen and slipped out the back way.

Feeling like one of her paparazzi-dodging, VIP patients, she trotted away from the clot of news media on her porch and toward the local convenience store.

A few minutes later, the cowbell over the door of the Stop and Shop clanked as Julie stepped over the threshold.

Head down, she hustled over to the magazine rack. Roped stacks of the *Inquisitive Tattler* lay on the floor. The shop clerk hadn't gotten around to unbundling them yet.

The front cover sent dread through her body. There she and Sebastian were. Lip-locked. Naked—although the picture only depicted them from the shoulders up. On the massage table in the Confidential Rejuvenations massage room. It looked as if the picture had been taken with an infrared, night-vision camera. Someone had been watching them making love. Julie's eyes were closed and she had the look of supreme ecstasy on her face.

The headline read Confidential Rejuvenations' Hollywood Spin Doctor Seduces Colin Cruz's Sex Therapist in Night of Sinful Passion.

"NO COMMENT," Sebastian told the microphone-wielding reporters flanking the front gate at Confidential Rejuvenations.

The minute he'd heard about the tabloid story, he'd rushed over to Julie's apartment only to find her place under siege by the media. When he tried to call her, he only got her voice mail. He had to find her and protect her from prying reporters.

Then his own phone had rung with Dr. Butler on the other end. Confidential Rejuvenations' chief of staff issued a terse, "Black, get over here right away."

Butler was mad, but Sebastian wasn't concerned for himself. All he could think about was how the fallout was going to affect Julie. It was his fault. He should have known better. He should have been more cautious.

He walked into Butler's office, his mind desperately searching for ways to spin this thing.

"Sit down, Black," Butler commanded. He held a copy of the *Inquisitive Tattler* in his fist.

Disturbed by the look in the man's eyes, Sebastian sat.

"I can't begin to tell you how unprofessional this kind of behavior is." Butler thumped the cover of the magazine.

"Sir, Julie and I were set up. Someone lured us to the tranquility gardens. I'm pretty sure the same person who was behind the Colin Cruz thing is the one who orchestrated this," he said.

"That's no excuse," Butler thundered. "Even if someone did lure you to the gardens, you were the one who exhibited poor judgment with this public display."

"That's the thing, it wasn't a public display until the saboteur decided to make it one."

"Now that I've expressed my disapproval," Butler went on, "I want you to know that since that gossip rag hit the stands we've had nonstop calls from people wanting to be admitted for rehab."

"Excuse me?"

Butler stopped pacing and sat down across from Sebastian. "Apparently, your…um…" He cleared his throat. "Indiscretion with Julie DeMarco in the tranquility garden has made rehab at Confidential Rejuvenations trendy."

"You're kidding."

"I guess it's true what they say. Bad publicity is better than no publicity at all."

"So this means…?"

Before Butler could answer, there was a knock at the door. "Come in," the chief of staff called out.

Tanner Doyle entered. "Dr. Butler," he said. "I know who's been sabotaging the hospital."

AS JULIE WAS HEADED for Dr. Butler's office to throw herself on his mercy and beg for her job, she saw him walking out with Sebastian and Tanner. The minute she met Sebastian's eyes, the courage that had gotten her this far evaporated.

"Wh-what's happened?"

Sebastian took her arm. "Tanner's caught the saboteur on camera. We're on our way down to his office to view the tape now."

Julie glanced at Butler. "May I go with you?"

Butler nodded curtly. She wondered if she was going to lose her job.

Sebastian tightened his grip on her arm, letting her know he was there for her. She took comfort in his presence, but she knew she couldn't rely on him. Once Sebastian cleaned up this mess, he'd go back to his life in L.A.

Sadness curled in her chest. Resolutely, she pushed it

away. She'd known from the beginning of this affair that she and Sebastian could never be more than temporary lovers. It was enough. He'd made it clear he was a guy who preferred to keep his options open and that was okay with her. She wasn't looking to get hitched. All she'd wanted was to overcome her sexual naïveté. To learn how to separate love from sex so she didn't end up getting her heart broken again like she had with Phillip and Roger.

They arrived in Tanner's office and he had them sit down while he flicked on the television monitor on his wall and hit the play button on the video recorder. "This is from the private spy camera I installed. It's not hooked up into our main system," he explained. "It's a good thing, too, because last night, the power to the main security cameras went off for half an hour. Watch this and you'll see why."

The screen filled with the picture of Confidential Rejuvenations' ivy-twined employee entrance on the east side of the building.

Tanner fast-forwarded it a bit as the camera caught people coming and going at the eleven o'clock shift change. The camera clock showed 11:25 p.m. and Julie saw herself appear on camera.

She sucked in her breath.

Sebastian reached over to squeeze her hand.

She watched herself on screen walk down the flagstone path toward the tranquility gardens headed for her rendezvous with Sebastian. Then she quickly disappeared out of the camera's range.

The camera fixed on the entrance. No one else came or went. Tanner fast-forwarded again, then hit the play button once more. Seconds later, the entrance door opened and Maxine Woodbury appeared. She glanced left, then right.

When she'd satisfied herself no one was around, she took something from her oversize purse.

Bolt cutters.

She sidled up to the metal box attached to the side of the building. It was almost hidden by the ivy. She pushed the ivy back, clipped the lock on the box and opened it.

"That's the box where the lines come in that control the main security cameras," Tanner explained. "And here's where she removes the relay."

Maxine monkeyed with something inside the box, then she stepped back, took her cell phone from her pocket and placed a call. Minutes later, she was joined by a squat balding man with a camera.

"That's one of the paparazzi who interviewed me after the Colin Cruz incident," Sebastian said.

"It's Maxine Woodbury?" Dr. Butler sounded stunned. "Maxine is the saboteur?"

Tanner nodded.

"Get her in here," Dr. Butler said. "I want an explanation and I want it now."

"YES," MAXINE SAID with a haughty toss of her head when Dr. Butler confronted her with the evidence. "I pulled the relay out of the box on the security cameras so the photographer could gain access to the grounds."

"But why?" Butler demanded. "You've been with this hospital for fifteen years, Maxine. You won employee of the year in 2006. Why would you want to destroy our hospital?"

In spite of the older woman's defiant attitude, Julie could see a glimmer of tears in her eyes. "Because," Maxine said, "you forced my hand."

"What are you talking about?" Butler frowned.

Maxine's chin quivered. "Earlier this year I got a letter, signed by you, I might add. It said I had to take mandatory retirement when I turned seventy. You were putting me out to pasture. It's not fair. I still have plenty of good years left in me and look how well I've kept up with technology. Yet when I came to you and asked if you could make an exception in my case, you told me that I'd earned a rest and you were sending me on a Caribbean cruise for a retirement present."

Butler looked confused. "Most people would love a Caribbean cruise."

"Floating funeral parlors! That's all they are," she scoffed. "So I figured if I couldn't stay here, I'd bring you down with me."

"The tabloid leaks, the kitchen fire, the thefts, the transformer and generator outages, the sliced tires in the employee parting lot?"

"All me." She proudly chuffed out her chest. "How's that for too old? I've been getting away with it for months and none of you ever suspected me."

"And Chloe?" Tanner asked about the scrub nurse who'd stabbed him. "Did you set her off?"

"Please." Maxine waved a hand. "That girl was a keg of dynamite. All I had to do was light the match and watch her explode. I had no idea she was going to stab you, though. I am sorry about that. I never wanted anyone to get hurt. I just wanted to ruin the hospital's reputation. Let you all see what it was like to have the thing you loved most destroyed."

"That was pretty selfish of you," Sebastian said.

She glowered at him. "Please, like you're Mr. Altruistic. If you hadn't been so good at lying, I could have finished off this place with Colin Cruz. But you..." She shook her head. "You're too damned slick."

Tanner looked at Dr. Butler. "You want me to call the police?"

Dr. Butler shook his head. "No. Just escort her off the premises. Losing her job will be punishment enough."

"WHAT HAPPENS NOW?" Julie asked Sebastian as they left the hospital together.

"About Maxine?"

"About our picture on the front page of the tabloid."

"I'll find a way to spin this so you're not left embarrassed by that *Inquisitive Tattler* story," he said. "Maybe I can say we were trying to trap Maxine and we went with it, knowing all along we were being photographed."

"Don't lie on my account."

"It's not lying it's..." He broke off. "It is lying, isn't it?"

She nodded.

It crushed down on him all at once. He'd made a profession out of bending the truth and telling people what they wanted to hear whether it was honest or not. Looking into Julie's eyes he suddenly felt like the world's biggest fraud.

"When are you going back to L.A.?" she asked.

"Not until Monday," he said. "My brother's engagement party is this coming Saturday."

"Oh."

"You could come to the party with me," he said. "I need a date."

"I don't know if that's such a good idea. After last night maybe we should just make a clean break."

He stared at her lips and had an overwhelming urge to kiss her. "I'd like you to meet my brother."

"For what purpose?"

"Excuse me?"

"You're going back to L.A. I live here and we both know you're a confirmed bachelor. What would be the point?"

"I'd like one last night with you, Julie," he said. "Is that so wrong?"

She blew out a breath.

His gaze tracked to the pale, snowy scope of skin between her diamond-studded earlobes and her slender collarbone. He'd never known a collarbone could be so sexy.

"They're having the engagement party in the ballroom of the hotel Shangri-La. It's formal. They're pulling out all the stops. We could get a room for the night. Soak in the hot tub. Have breakfast in bed. Our last tango so to speak."

She said nothing.

Sebastian shrugged, trying to appear nonchalant. "Just a thought. I'm sure you don't want to dress up fancy and dance the night away like Cinderella."

Julie canted her head and looked at him. Was the woman ever going to say anything?

"You probably wouldn't feel comfortable meeting my brother and his fiancée and my secretary, Blanche, and my nutty Aunt Bunnie and her friends from the commune, I understand. Engagement parties and weddings make me nervous, too."

"Sebastian…I…" She licked out her tongue to moisten her lip and it was all he could do to keep from groaning.

"So this is goodbye then?" He forced himself to smile, unable to decipher why his chest felt so damn tight. He couldn't get any air. Why couldn't he get some air?

It's just because she's so hot and sexy. Julie is the best you've ever had. That's all it is. This feeling will pass and you'll be on to the next woman.

He reached up to loosen his tie.

Okay, so she was more special than most, but what did he have to offer her really beyond a good time?

She was a forever kind of woman and he was a freedom-loving guy. She deserved far more than he had the capacity to give. She was right, going with him to the engagement party was a bad idea. He didn't know why he'd even suggested it.

He had to get out of here. If she was ready to call it quits then the sooner he left, the better. "I gotta go, Jules…." He cleared his throat. "Julie."

"Sebastian." Her eyes were fixed on his.

He couldn't fricking breathe. He snatched off his tie. "Yes?"

"I'll go."

JULIE DRESSED FOR the engagement party with much thought and attention to detail. She knew this was her last hoorah with Sebastian and she wanted to make it a night to remember.

Plus, she had an ulterior motive for attending. Sebastian's brother was engaged to Keeley Marshall, the daughter of her ex-lover. This was the perfect opportunity to show Roger how much she'd grown. Prove to him and herself that he hadn't destroyed her. She was going to that party and holding her head high. The trick was to keep Sebastian from finding out that Roger was her ex-lover.

She'd spent a small fortune on a new outfit for the event, shopping at Neiman Marcus for a black-and-white strapless cocktail dress that hugged her hourglass figure and exposed her shoulders and the top of her breasts. Plus, she'd splurged on designer stilettos and a black-and-white beaded handbag. She also spritzed on a fresh, new cologne called Sassy. It smelled of cinnamon, ginger and licorice. The frisky scent underscored her adventuresome mood. She completed the ensemble with a black-and-white bracelet and matching earrings. Finally, she twisted her hair up in an Audrey Hepburn–style French twist, anchoring it in place with a black-and-white butterfly hairpin.

She stared at herself in the mirror, unable to believe the change in her appearance. She hadn't been this elegantly attired since her high school prom. Come to think of it, her neon pink prom dress hadn't exactly been haute couture.

The look in Sebastian's eyes when he came to pick her up told her that she'd scored big. "Wow," he said. "I'm going to have the best-looking date in the place."

They arrived at the hotel Shangri-La at seven and Sebastian tossed the keys to the valet, then hurried around to the passenger side of the car to offer her his arm.

He escorted her over to one side. "Before we go in…" He took a white oblong box from his jacket pocket. "I wanted to give you a small memento of our time together."

Julie's heart skipped a beat. "Is this what you do for all your conquests?" she teased, even though she was feeling anything but jovial. "Buy them a parting gift?"

His eyes darkened. "You're not a conquest."

With one finger, she plucked at the red ribbon, untying it and then lifted the lid. Inside, nestled on tissue paper, lay a platinum medallion on a matching chain.

"Oh, Sebastian." She inhaled and took the necklace from the box. The medallion was an eagle in flight. Just like the regal bird on his shoulder tattoo. "It's beautiful."

He shrugged and looked adorably embarrassed. "Turn around and I'll put it on for you."

She handed him the medallion, turned, lifted her hair. His

warm fingers went around, the medallion lay cool against her bare skin.

After he hooked the clasp, he pressed his mouth to her ear and whispered, “Fly free, Jules, fly free.”

12

FLY FREE INDEED.

She was here to face Roger and put her past to rest, but the minute she saw him in the ballroom, icy fingers of fear gripped her. She wanted to turn and run, but Sebastian held fast to her elbow as he tugged her toward the tall blond man in a tuxedo standing beside Roger. She couldn't bear the shame if Sebastian learned Roger was her ex-lover.

"Julie, I want you to meet my brother, Lincoln Holt. Linc, this is my date, Julie DeMarco."

Julie shook hands with Sebastian's brother. Then Sebastian introduced her to his secretary. Blanche Santini had kind eyes and a wise face. She was dressed in a two-piece suit reminiscent of Jacqueline Kennedy.

"I've heard so much about you," Blanche said.

"Really?" Julie shot a glance at Sebastian.

"Julie," Lincoln said, "I want you to meet my fiancée, Keeley."

Keeley. Roger's daughter.

It was all Julie could do to smile and look the dark-haired girl in the eye. "Congratulations on your engagement."

"Thank you." Keeley returned her smile.

She felt like the biggest Benedict Arnold on the planet. She'd slept with this girl's father. Shame burned her.

Keeley rested an arm on the woman beside her. "This is my mother, Margery."

Roger's wife.

Guilt gripped her. Without meaning to do so, she'd wronged this woman. She shouldn't have come here. She should have thought this thing through. She'd wanted to face down Roger, she hadn't expected to have to face his wife as well.

Margery said, "I'm pleased to meet you."

Julie could only nod. *Keep up the facade. Don't let anyone know. Especially Sebastian.*

Keeley touched Roger's shoulder. "And this is my father, Roger Marshall."

"Mr. Marshall," she said tightly.

Roger reached out and took her hand. Julie stared at his bow tie, not wanting to look him in the face. He pressed his lips to the back of her hand, essentially flirting with her right in front of his wife and daughter. How had she ever thought she cared for this man? "It's a pleasure."

She stiffened and pulled her hand away as discreetly as she could. She longed to tell Roger to go straight to hell, but of course she couldn't do that.

"If you'll excuse me," she said. "I think I've got something in my eye."

Without another word, she turned and fled to the ladies' room. She plunked onto the sofa in the lounge area, sucking in big gulps of air and trying to calm herself.

A few minutes later, Blanche wandered in and sat down beside her. "Are you all right?"

"No."

Blanche slipped an arm around her. "Do you want to tell me what's bothering you?"

"I had an affair with Keeley's father," she blurted. "I didn't know he was married, I swear I didn't, but I feel so wretched. What have I done?"

"You made a mistake."

"I didn't even know I was making one."

Blanche took a clean tissue from her pocket and passed it to her, and it was only then Julie realized she was crying. "I keep making horrible mistakes when it comes to men."

"Is Sebastian one of those mistakes?"

Julie nodded and dabbed at the tears.

"I don't think Sebastian is a mistake."

"What?" Sniffling, Julie looked at the older woman.

"I've seen the women come and the women go in his life and Sebastian has never looked at a single one of them the way he looks at you."

"Really?" A stupid surge of hope took hold of her.

"He's smitten."

"He's not. He's told me repeatedly he's a confirmed bachelor."

"The man's terrified of getting hurt. His mother died when he was a kid and his father never recognized him. Sebastian won't admit it, but it's had an impact on who he is. He's scared of loving, terrified of losing someone he cares about. He thinks if he keeps his emotions out of it, that he won't fall." Blanche laughed a knowing laugh. "As if you can control love."

Love?

Julie's heart lurched. Could it be true? Did she dare hope that she meant more to Sebastian than a short-term affair? And what if he did care? Did she really want to be with a man who had trouble with commitment? She'd had enough of dead-end romances. She didn't want to go down that road again.

"You could be the one to bring him to his knees." Blanche shifted on the seat beside her.

"How do you know that?"

"Because when he called me every night to check in on the business, he talked about you. He's never, ever talked to me about his girlfriends."

"I'm not his girlfriend."

"If you say so." She shrugged.

"He talked about me? Every night?"

Blanche nodded. "And he invited you to his brother's engagement party. A man doesn't invite just anyone to meet his family and friends."

She wanted to believe Blanche, she really did, but the medallion at her throat was sending a completely different message.

"Come on." Blanche got to her feet and extended her hand to help Julie up. "They'll be serving dinner soon and we don't want to miss out."

"YOU'RE DIFFERENT," Linc told Sebastian.

"Huh?" Sebastian's gaze was fixed on the door of the ladies' room. What was taking Blanche so long? Was something wrong with Julie? Anxiety knotted his stomach.

"Yeah." Linc canted his head. "You look…"

Sighing, he ran a hand through his hair. "Like what?"

"Like the rest of us."

He met his brother's eyes. "What's that supposed to mean?"

"You look humbled."

"Getting caught in a compromising position on the front page of the *Inquisitive Tattler* will do that to you."

"Nope." Lincoln shook his head. "That's not it."

"No?"

"I think it's got more to do with who you got caught on the cover with."

"Julie?" He tried to sound casual, but damn if his voice didn't rise when he said her name.

"She's changed you."

"No way. I've only known her three weeks."

"Love has no time limit."

Love?

Just the mention of the word had his heart thumping and his palms sweating and his throat tightening. "I'm not in love."

"You can run, but you can't hide."

"You're just besotted with Keeley and you think everyone should couple up."

"Actually I do, but that's because I want you to feel what I feel, brother. You deserve love."

Sebastian snorted, but his throat constricted tighter and his nose burned. *Not in love, I'm not in love.*

And then he saw Julie emerging from the bathroom with Blanche and his heart leapt. He felt a silly grin eat up his face and he started across the room toward her.

But before Sebastian could reach her, Roger Marshall stepped up to her, leaned in close and whispered something in her ear. Julie's eyes widened at whatever it was he'd said to her. She nodded, waved at Blanche and then turned to follow Roger out into the corridor.

Where were they going? Why was she leaving the ballroom with him?

He hadn't liked the way Roger Marshall had looked at her from the minute they were introduced. And that hand-kissing thing. What the hell had that been about?

Jealousy sent him after them.

"Seb?" Lincoln called, but he didn't turn around.

He slipped out into the hallway, the doors automatically closing behind him drowning out strains of the band playing party music. He looked up and down the plush, carpeted corridor and heard murmured voices coming from an alcove. Blood pounding through his veins, he approached the alcove, intent on eavesdropping.

"I've missed you so much, Julie," Roger was saying.

"You're married, Roger, I have no interest in taking up where we left off."

Sebastian felt as if he'd been kicked in the heart by an elephant. Roger Marshall was the married man Julie had had an affair with? He gasped, unable to pull in air. He couldn't believe it.

"I'm leaving Margery," Roger declared.

"It doesn't matter. I don't want you. You lied to me. You cheated on your wife. You're not a man worth having."

"It's that Sebastian Black, isn't it? Well, you're kidding yourself if you think a guy like him would ever want you."

"Please take your hands off me, Roger." Julie's voice was sharp enough to cut steel.

"Come on, baby, give me a kiss. I've been burning up for you since the minute you walked through the door."

"Let go of me, you bastard!"

One second Sebastian was standing outside the alcove and the next he was charging around the corner. Roger Marshall had Julie pinned up against the wall and he was trying to run his hand up under her skirt.

Sebastian heard someone bellow and it was only when his fist connected with Roger's face that he knew the noise had spilled from his own mouth.

Roger yelped and fell to his knees, raising both arms up to shield his face. "Don't hit me again," he whimpered.

"I ought to smash your teeth down your throat for the way you treated this woman." Sebastian stood over him, fists clenched, breathing like an enraged bull.

"Sebastian!" Linc called from behind him. "What are you doing?"

"Daddy?" Keeley warbled.

Sebastian closed his eyes when he recognized Keeley's voice. *Ah, shit. This wasn't going to end well.*

"Roger?"

At the sound of Margery Marshall's voice, Sebastian turned to see her standing beside Linc and Keeley. His gaze swung back to find Julie. She was struggling to look composed. He couldn't begin to imagine what she was feeling. He hurt for her and all she was suffering.

Margery started toward them.

Sebastian's eyes met Julie's. She looked utterly terrified. He stepped between Julie and Roger. The only way anyone was going to get to her was through his dead body.

Roger's lip was bleeding and he had a smear of what looked to be lipstick on his chin. "Call security, Margery. This man assaulted me."

But Margery Marshall was not a stupid woman. She walked right up to her husband, drew back her hand and slapped him hard across the face. "That's for cheating on me with a girl young enough to be your daughter."

Roger's hand went to his cheek.

"And as for you—" Margery glowered at Julie "—you should be ashamed of yourself, sleeping with a married man."

"I didn't know he was married. I swear. Please forgive me, Mrs. Marshall. I broke it off as soon as I found out."

"Daddy, how could you!" Keeley burst into tears and fled.

Linc glared at Sebastian. "I knew you were jealous of my happiness, Sebastian, but I never believed you could stoop to something this low."

Then his brother turned and went after his bride.

Margery pointed a finger at her husband. "I want you out of the house. Tonight. This marriage is over."

Roger staggered to his feet, wiping his mouth with the back of his hand. "You're going to pay for this," he told Julie. "I'll have your job."

Sebastian pulled back his fist. "You want me to smack you again? I'm happy to do it."

Roger spat a curse, but shambled off leaving only Sebastian and Julie in the alcove.

She wouldn't look at him and when he reached out a hand to touch her, she pulled away. "Please, Sebastian," she said. "Please, just leave me alone."

JULIE HAD THOUGHT getting her picture plastered on the front cover of the *Inquisitive Tattler* making love to Sebastian was humiliating, but until this moment, she hadn't known the true meaning of the word.

Mortified, she turned away from Sebastian, wobbling on her high-heeled shoes. She'd been a fool to come here. How stupid she'd been to think she could handle Roger. All she'd wanted to do was prove he no longer had a hold over her.

"Julie." Sebastian stood between her and the exit and he wasn't moving.

"Please go." She raised a hand to shield her face. "I've degraded myself enough for one evening."

"You have nothing to be ashamed of." He leaned in closer, rested his forearm on the wall above her head.

"You should go. See if you can smooth things over with your brother and Keeley."

"You're my date, I'm not going off and leaving you."

She didn't want him here, seeing her disgrace. "Go back to your party."

"The party's ruined."

"And it's all my fault," she wailed.

"Julie," he commanded, "look at me."

She raised her head and met his gaze. "What do you want from me, Sebastian?"

His eyes darkened. He looked as if he wanted to kiss her, to brand her as his own. But of course that was nonsense. She knew he wasn't interested in commitment. He'd told her so himself. More than once. She was foolish if she thought she could change him.

She'd been even more foolish to think she could change herself. Having a fling hadn't taken any of the stars from her eyes. She was just as wretchedly romantic as she'd ever been. Her grand experiment was a huge failure on all fronts.

"I want..." He swallowed visibly. "I want to be with you."

"In what capacity?"

"What do you mean?"

"In what capacity? Friend? Lover? Boyfriend?" *Husband?*

"I...I...don't know."

She straightened, stepped back from him. "Let me make this easy for you, Sebastian. Feel free to go home to L.A. Don't feel like you owe me anything. I don't need you to take care of me, or feel sorry for me. I know you don't do commitment. That's the very reason I started an affair with you in the first place."

"What do you mean?"

"I was trying to get over Roger. I'd just flunked my exam to become certified as a sex therapist. I was in limbo. I needed adventure and I needed casual sex and then you walked into my life and you fit the bill. It was perfect. Don't go ruining it now by trying to make it anything more than it was. We had a good time. Let it go at that."

He couldn't have looked more stunned if she'd slapped him the way Margery had slapped Roger.

"But you taught me something very important about myself and I thank you for that."

"Wh-what did I teach you?" He seemed utterly confused.

"That I'm a romantic at heart. That I want the husband, the house, the kids in the yard, the white picket fence, a dog named Rover and a cat named Fluffy. I'm not like you. I can't separate love from sex. It goes against who I am."

"Oh."

"Yeah." She nodded and a chill chased up her spine. "Oh."

If they were in a movie, this would be the part where he would tell her he wanted all those things, too. Then he would take her in his arms and kiss her and tell her that he wanted to spend the rest of his life with her.

But of course, he didn't do that.

"So you used me to get Roger out of your system," he said flatly.

"I did," she admitted. "I'm not proud of myself."

"Did it work at least?"

"Yes, it did. And that's what I really have to thank you for." She reached up and wrapped her hand around the medallion at her neck. "You set me free, Sebastian, to be who I'm supposed to be."

His expression was bone-chilling. "You're welcome, Julie. I hope you get everything you want."

Then he turned and walked away, shattering her heart cleanly in two.

JULIE.

Sebastian couldn't stop thinking about her. She'd cast a spell over him. He didn't even know who he was anymore. He kept having these thoughts that belonged to a different kind of man. Thoughts of marriage and kids and happily-ever-after. He kept imagining what it might be like to lead a different life. To sell his Beverly Hills mansion and give up doctoring the truth for a living.

No matter how hard he tried, he couldn't shake her. She was an infection, slipping through his veins, burning up his brain.

Worst of all, he couldn't sleep.

Ever since he'd returned to his home in Beverly Hills nothing seemed the same. His house was big and empty. The parties he attended superfluous. Even driving his Ferrari no longer boosted his mood.

To counter the effects of Julie withdrawal, he threw himself into his favorite activities. Surfing, going to Lakers games, hitting the clubs two or three nights a week with a new woman on his arm each time. But nothing salved the loneliness.

Three weeks after the fiasco at the Shangri-La, Sebastian trudged into his office. Blanche brought him an espresso and placed a white envelope on his desk.

He looked up at her. "What's this?"

"My resignation."

"What?" He stared. "You can't quit." Blanche was the

only constant in his life. She took care of him and kept him in line. Losing her would be like losing his left arm.

"I'm sorry, Sebastian," she said gently.

"Is it money? Whatever you want. Just name it. It's yours."

"I'm flattered that you think I'm worth so much." Her smile was soft. "But money isn't going to keep me here."

"Okay, I know I've been in a foul mood ever since I got back from Austin—"

"It's not your mood. Although, yes, you've been quite impossible."

"What is it then?"

Blanche's smile widened. "I'm getting married."

"What? When? To who?"

"To whom," she corrected.

"Grammar Nazi."

"And you wonder why I'm handing in my resignation."

"So whom is this dude?"

Blanche rolled her eyes. "You and that foul mood again."

"The guy that you're leaving me for. When did this happen? What's his name?"

"His name is Brian Weatherly and I met him while you were in Austin."

"So you've known him, what? Six weeks at most?"

She folded her arms over her chest. "Something like that."

"Do I get to meet him?"

"Yes. You're invited to dinner at my house tonight."

"I don't get it. How can you fall in love with a guy you've only known six weeks?"

"I've learned a few things in my fiftysomething years on the planet. For one thing, life is preciously short and you need to grab all the happiness you can stuff into your fists. And when it comes to love, real, true and lasting love, you know when you've found it. With my Edward, I'd only known him two weeks when he asked me to marry him. Time is irrelevant."

"You're serious."

"We're moving to Sedona. I've always wanted to live there. You're invited to the wedding of course. It's on Christmas Eve at my sister's house in Long Beach."

Sebastian shook his head. "Blanche and Brian. It's too cutesy."

"You're only upset because you're going to have to train a new secretary."

"No," he said. "I'm upset because I'm losing my best friend."

Blanche blinked. "Don't you dare make me cry. You're not losing me, I just won't be taking care of you anymore. Besides, it's time you found a best friend your own age."

He had found one his own age, but he'd gone off and left her in Austin, Texas.

"Linc's getting married and moving away and now you. I've got nothing left," he said as much to himself as to Blanche.

"You could have Julie."

"Julie doesn't want me."

"Are you seriously that dumb?"

"Come on, she told me she'd only used me as a rebound relationship to help her get over Roger."

"She said that because she was terrified you'd reject her if she told you what she really wanted, so she pretended you meant nothing more to her than a roll in the hay."

His pulse quickened. "You think so?"

"Sebastian, are you blind? That girl's so madly in love with you she can't think straight. Now, if you don't need me for anything else, I'll be cleaning out my desk."

He followed Blanche into the reception area. “You really think Julie’s in love with me?”

“Why don’t you go ask her yourself?”

13

"WANNA GO FOR PIZZA?" Elle asked.

Julie shook her head and opened her locker. "You guys go on without me."

"How can we go without you?" Vanessa wheedled. "We're celebrating you passing your certifying exam. It's official, you're a sex therapist. That calls for pizza and beer."

"I put in for a transfer back to newborn nursery," she told her friends and hung up her stethoscope.

"Why?" Vanessa asked.

And Elle added, "You finally pass the test and now you want out?"

Julie shrugged. "I realize I don't want to be a sex therapist."

"After all that hard work?" Vanessa handed Julie her coat. "What happened?"

"It's not me. I came to this unit to prove to myself I could handle the reality of sex. I came, I saw, I conquered. I'm ready to move on."

"Just like with Sebastian," Elle asked.

"Exactly like with Sebastian."

"He was a firecracker." Vanessa picked up her purse.

"And firecrackers always burn out." Julie hardened her chin and the memories that assailed her every time she thought of Sebastian.

"He was so good-looking." Elle sighed.

"We have completely different values." Julie took off her nursing clogs and slipped into her cowboy boots. It was the same speech she gave herself every night for the past three weeks as she battled insomnia.

After having her sexual appetite whetted by his incredible lovemaking it had been pretty damned hard going back to her quiet little life. She'd taken all that excess energy and channeled it into studying for her exam. It had paid off, but now that she had the certificate in her hand, the victory felt hollow. She had to find a new goal in a vain attempt to keep the ghosts at bay.

How long was it going to take her to get over him? Two months? Six months? A year?

Julie shivered. What if she never got over him? What if she spent her life mooning over yet another unobtainable man?

"Come on." Elle slipped her arm through Julie's. "You're going for pizza and beer whether you want to or not."

"Yeah," Vanessa said. "You've learned you can live through the worst and survive. We're here for you. Whatever you need."

They were right. Sebastian had taught her some valuable lessons and her friends were here to help her pick up the pieces. What more did she need?

"Besides," Elle said as they walked toward the elevator, arm in arm, "who says you and Sebastian can't work things out."

"Please, he's a playboy."

"Hey, even they settle down eventually."

"I'm not holding my breath."

Vanessa punched the button for the elevator. "You two did look really happy on the front cover of the *Inquisitive Tattler.*"

Julie groaned. "Did you have to bring that up? People finally have stopped asking me about it."

"I'm just saying, you did have some good times."

"Good times do not a lifetime make."

"There's not the slightest chance you two could work this out?" Elle asked.

"He hasn't called me in three weeks."

"Have you called him?"

"No, of course not." Julie reached up to finger the eagle medallion at her throat. And then the tears she'd been denying so long welled up in her eyes.

"Jules, are you crying?" Elle sounded alarmed.

"No." She sniffled.

Vanessa plucked a tissue from her pocket and passed it to her. "Let it out, sweetie."

The tears trickling down her face as they stood in the elevator told her she hadn't fully dealt with what had happened. She'd thrown herself into studying for her test and tried to ignore her emotions. She would survive this. She would forget all about Sebastian Black.

She rubbed away the tears. "Let's go get that pizza and beer."

SEBASTIAN PULLED IN TO the parking lot at Confidential Rejuvenations at eleven-fifteen at night, not even sure what he was going to say to Julie when he saw her. He'd taken Blanche's advice, gone straight to LAX, bought a ridiculously overpriced last-minute fare and flown to Austin without a plan in his head.

He got out of his rental car just as Elle and Vanessa and Julie came walking out of the employee entrance.

Julie saw him and stopped walking.

Elle and Vanessa kept going, mumbling good-night, and climbed into their cars and motored off, leaving him and Julie standing alone in the cool night air underneath the streetlamp.

She was dressed in a black turtleneck sweater, black slacks, tweed jacket and black cowboy boots.

"Julie," he whispered and went toward her, his heart pounding erratically.

"Hey there, cowboy." The sound of her voice reached out and wrapped around him like a hug.

He couldn't talk, could only stare and stare and stare. He could stare at her all night and never get enough of looking at her.

Her hair was loose and tumbling about her shoulders in silky waves. She was wearing the platinum eagle medallion he'd given her. She looked poised and relaxed and utterly beautiful.

"Sebastian, what are you doing here?"

"I came to see you."

"I can see that."

God, how he wanted to gather her up in his arms and tell her, really tell her how he felt. But he was new at this. Had never said the words before and he didn't know how to start. "Julie…"

"How's Lincoln and Keeley?"

"They had a rough patch after that night at the engagement party. Keeley went through a crisis of faith in the wake of her parents' breakup, but Linc gave her the space she needed and they worked things out."

"So the wedding's still on?"

"Yeah. They really love each other."

"That's wonderful."

"What about Roger?" he asked.

"I heard through the grapevine he and Margery are going through with the divorce. She threw him out."

"I know about that. Keeley told me. What about *you* and Roger?" he asked, terrified to hear the answer.

"There is no me and Roger. There never really was except in my imagination. He was a married man and I was nothing but a dalliance for him."

"And I was nothing but a salve for your ego."

Julie drew in her breath. "In the beginning, yes, but…"

"But what?"

"I'm not ready to go there."

"Why not?"

"You took off on me, Sebastian."

"You told me to leave you alone."

She caught her bottom lip between her teeth. "True."

A long silence stretched between them. This wasn't going the way he'd imagined on the plane. They were both feeling their way through this.

"Whatever happened to Maxine?" he asked while he tried to figure out exactly how to say what was in his heart.

"She's answering phones for the *Inquisitive Tattler,*" Julie replied.

"Confidential Rejuvenations should have pressed charges," he said, "but they didn't want bad PR."

Her gaze searched his face. "How are things in the spin-doctor business?"

"Not so good."

"No?"

He came closer. With each step his pulse thudded harder, swifter. "I'm thinking maybe it's time I tried a new career."

"Honestly?"

"You gave me a lot to think about and I realized maybe it's not the most honorable profession in the world."

"What will you do instead?"

"I don't know," he admitted. But he wasn't worried about that. He had plenty of options.

"You came to this conclusion after Colin Cruz had another meltdown? Where was it they caught him having sex this time?"

"The roller coaster on the Stratosphere in Vegas. You heard about that?"

"It was all over the *Inquisitive Tattler.*"

"You were right about him. He needed help. And you were right about me. I did him a disservice."

"So *you're* having a crisis of faith."

"Maybe. But it goes deeper than Colin Cruz."

"How's that?"

"Blanche quit on me."

"Oh?"

"She's getting married."

"Good for her. I like Blanche."

"So do I. She's why I'm here by the way." He took another step. She didn't back up, but neither did she hurry to close the distance between them.

"Blanche sent you?"

"Uh-huh." Another step. If he reached out his arm he could slide it around her waist.

Her eyes were fixed on his. "Why did she send you?"

"To ask you a question."

"What question is that?"

Sebastian took a deep breath. Was he really ready to say the words?

If not now, then you'll never be ready.

Sebastian looked into Julie's eyes and he just knew it was the right thing to do. Never mind his doubts. Never mind the way he used to be. Never mind the life he was leaving behind. There was a whole new life waiting for him if he was willing to reach out and grab the opportunity.

One more step and the tips of his shoes where butted up against the tips of her cowboy boots. "Blanche says you're in love with me, is that true?"

She tilted her head up at him. "You came all this way to ask me that? You could have made a phone call. It would have been much cheaper."

"Just answer the question."

"No."

"No?" Sudden panic seized him. Blanche was wrong. Julie didn't love him! Impossible pain seared through his heart.

"No, I'm not going to answer your question. I'm tired of being the one to put my heart on the line for a relationship. If you want me, you've got to tell me."

"I want you," he growled.

"In what capacity? Friend? Lover? Boyfriend?"

"All of the above."

A light of hope flickered in her eyes. She was just as scared as he was.

"What happened to flying free?"

"It's garbage. Just something I told myself to justify my lifestyle and my fear of commitment."

"So what's changed?"

"After I went back home, I tried to pick up where I'd left off, but I couldn't do it. I tried to forget you, but I simply couldn't get you out of my head or my heart."

She looked like she wanted to believe him. "Are you sure I'm the one?"

"Julie DeMarco, I've never been more certain of anything in my life."

"But I don't understand. You could have anyone. Models, actresses, singers, dancers. Why me? Why now?"

"Other than the fact I'm madly in love with you?"

Julie inhaled sharply.

"Yes, I said it. I love you. I love you for your bright-eyed optimism and your fierce loyalty to your patients and your values. I love you because you're a crazy mix of innocent and wild. Of sweet and sexy. Because you have a giving heart and a kind soul. I'm crazy about the paradox that's you. But most of all, I love you because being with you makes me a better man."

"But I've done some bad things. Made a lot of mistakes."

"And you think I haven't?" He couldn't stand not touching her one minute longer. He put his arm around her waist and pulled her flush against his body. She didn't resist and that gave him courage. "Woman, I give thanks for the mistakes we've both made because it's turned us into the people we are today. Don't you get it? I think you're beautiful just the way you are. Flaws and all. And I hope you can accept me for my imperfections as well."

Sebastian splayed his hand over her heart. "I love what's inside here."

Tears misted her eyes. "But you left. You never called."

"Because I was scared to death of these feelings. I'd never felt them before, Julie. You gotta remember, this is all new to me."

"You've never been in love before?"

"Never. I mean here I was, a guy who's spent his life running from relationships. I'd convinced myself love was a trap. I was stone-cold terrified to admit I'd been wrong. I thought commitment meant the end of fun and freedom. Lincoln tried to tell me what I was missing, but I couldn't understand until it happened to me. Imagine, I was falling madly in love with you, and I find out you had a thing with Roger and then you told me you were only using me to get over him and I…" His throat clotted with emotion and he couldn't continue.

"I hurt your feelings."

"Hurt, hell, I felt like you'd ripped out my insides and stomped on them."

"I was afraid to admit I was falling in love with another unobtainable man."

"I can see that now."

"How do you know for sure this is real?"

"Because when I went back to my old life, I took out women. A different one every night. I went to clubs. I raced my Ferrari down the Pacific Coast Highway. It all felt so meaningless. The joy was gone. Without you, everything seemed so empty. I realized I'd been filling my life with glitz and glamour to keep from seeing what wasn't there."

"And what's that?"

"Love."

Julie smiled. In Sebastian's face, she saw the vulnerable man beneath the charming facade. She knew this was not easy for him. That he was really going out on a limb. She stared into his black eyes and what she saw reflected in those dark depths moved her deeply and allowed her to let go of any lingering doubt. This declaration of love wasn't impulsive or casual. He meant what he was saying.

Her pulse rate, which had been bounding through her veins ever since she'd spied him in the parking lot looking a little lost and hesitant, finally slowed to a normal rhythm as her man dipped his head and whispered, "I love you, Julie. Now and forever and always. This isn't a game. It's not just about sex. It's real. You can count on that and you can count on me."

For a starry-eyed romantic, he said exactly what she needed to hear most. The wide-eyed girl who'd spent her life planning her wedding and daydreaming of Mr. Right felt it all come together. Her deepest fantasies had finally come true.

"Oh, Sebastian, I love you, too," she murmured.

"I want it all, Jules. You, the house, the kids, the white picket fence. However, there are a couple of other things I want to iron out first," he said.

A skitter of anxiety ran through her. "What is it?" she asked breathlessly.

"Do we have to name the dog Rover? Because I'm really partial to Spot."

She laughed and all her fears completely blew away. He was teasing her. His sense of humor was one of the things she loved most about him. "Spot it is."

"And I'm allergic to cats, so I hope that isn't a deal breaker." He wrapped his arms tightly around her.

"What about hamsters?"

"Hamsters are good."

"Hamster it is then."

"You know what?"

"What?"

"I'd kiss you, but I have a feeling we're being watched."

"Huh?"

She turned to look over her shoulder to see that they were standing right in the path of one of the parking lot scanning surveillance cameras. "Hey, after we made the cover of the *In-*

quisitive Tattler everyone at Confidential Rejuvenations knows we're exhibitionists. So to heck with them. Kiss me anyway."

"And risk lethal exposure?"

"The only thing that's lethal is what's going to happen if you don't kiss me."

"Gotcha," he said.

Then, camera be damned, Sebastian kissed her.

Epilogue

"THE STICK TURNED BLUE. How are you planning on spinning your way out of this one, Sebastian?" Julie teased.

Sebastian looked up from painting the walls of their new home on the banks of the Colorado River to see his wife standing in the hallway, a pregnancy-test kit in her hand. "What?"

A huge grin spread across her face. "We're pregnant. Happy?"

He tossed the paintbrush in the tray and rushed across the room to take her in his arms. "Wildly. Who shall we call first? Your mom? Blanche? Elle and Dante? Vanessa and Tanner?"

"Whoa," she said as he scooped her into his arms and spun her around the room. "It's a little premature for announcements. I just skipped my period."

"But I want everyone to know," he said, the warmth of utter happiness suffusing him from the inside out.

"You can tell them. All in good time."

The glow in her eyes caught him low in the belly and flamed his passion the way it always did when she looked at him like that. Julie made him feel like five kinds of hero.

How on earth had he ever believed love and marriage was a trap? In six weeks of marriage, he'd had more fun than he'd had in all the previous thirty years and it sounded as if things were really about to get exciting.

Imagine. A baby. His and Julie's baby. The thought turned him inside out with joy.

They had to consummate this moment. Burn it in their memories forever. He carried her to the bedroom and spread her on the new bed they'd recently bought for their new home. He'd sold his house in Beverly Hills, given up his PR business and bought a quarter share in Confidential Rejuvenations. He had lots of ideas for taking the hospital to a whole new level.

He looked down at her and his heart filled with so much love it hurt. He nestled his face against her neck, felt her pulse pounding at the hollow of her throat.

"Sebastian," Julie whispered and he decided there was no lovelier sound on earth than her voice, calling his name.

She smelled of vanilla and sweet, wonderful woman and her skin was silky soft beneath his fingers.

His blood ran feverishly hot. He wanted her so badly he couldn't stand himself. He wrestled out of his clothes, and peeled Julie out of hers.

She took his hand and guided him where she wanted him to go. He found her slick and ready and waiting for him. When he stroked her, she hissed in a breath. It constantly amazed him how receptive she was to his touch.

"Make love to me, Sebastian."

"Yes, ma'am."

He got to his feet, tugged her to the edge of the mattress while he stood on the floor between her spread legs. Greedily, he pushed into her, groaning as her sweet, slick heat encased him.

JULIE ARCHED HER BACK, raised her hips, pushed her body forward onto his steel shaft, welcoming his eager thrusts.

The poignancy of their union, on the day she'd found out she was having his baby, captured her mind and her heart. This is what she'd been searching for her entire life. This connection, this intimacy.

He looked into her eyes and she looked into his and they were one. She could feel his love for her as he poured himself into her body. This vast, wonderful, unconditional love.

More, more, she wanted more of him.

He matched her frantic rhythm and soon she felt the power of orgasm grip them both.

Simultaneously, wave after shuddering wave rippled through their joined bodies, lifting them together on joyous peaks of pleasure. A keen wail ripped through both their throats at the same time. Their sounds reverberated off the walls of the house where they were going to raise their baby and live their lives.

Sebastian collapsed on the bed beside her, and then drew her into his arms. She rested her head on his chest, listening to the pounding of his heart as he tightened his embrace around her.

"I love you so much, Julie," he murmured. "More than I ever thought possible."

She pressed her lips against his salty skin. "I love you, too, Sebastian."

For a long time, they stayed in the circle of each other's arms. Julie realized she'd never felt so complete, so wanted, so whole. He'd given her what she'd spent a lifetime searching for. True and honest love.

* * * * *

Her breath whistled out in a sigh of relief when he exited Customs. Devon recognized him right away from the newspaper and magazine articles her friend and partner Sabrina had looked up during her frantic prep work.

Caleb John Logan, Jr. Thirty-one. Six-two. With jet-black hair, laser-blue eyes and a linebacker's shoulders under his charcoal-gray cashmere overcoat. His jaw-dropping good looks didn't score him any points with Devon. She'd learned the hard way not to trust handsome heartbreakers like Cal Logan.

But he was a client. An important one. And she was willing to give someone who'd served a hitch in the marines before earning a B.S. from the University of Oregon, an MBA from Stanford and his first million at the ripe old age of twenty-six the benefit of the doubt.

Right up until he spotted the hot-pink pashmina, that is.

Devon knew the flash of color was more visible than the sign she held up with his name on it. So she wasn't surprised when Logan picked her out of the crowd and cut in her direction. She'd just plastered on her best businesswoman smile when he whipped an arm around her waist. The next moment she was sprawled against his cashmere-covered chest.

"Hello, brown eyes."

Swooping down, he covered her mouth with his.

Sheer astonishment kept Devon rooted to the spot for a few seconds while her mind whirled chaotically. Her first thought was that her client had downed a few too many drinks during the long flight. Her second, that he'd mistaken the kind of escort and consulting services her company provided. Her third shoved everything else out of her head.

The man could kiss!

His mouth moved over hers with a skill that ignited sparks at a half dozen flash points throughout her body. Devon hadn't experienced that kind of spontaneous combustion in a while. A *long* while.

The sparks were still popping when she pushed off his chest, only now they fueled a flush of anger.

"Do you always greet women you don't know with a liplock, Mr. Logan?"

A smile crinkled the skin at the corners of his eyes. "As a matter of fact, I don't. That was from Don."

"Huh?"

"He said he owed you one from New Year's Eve two years ago and made me promise to deliver it."

She stared up at him in total incomprehension. Logan hooked a brow and attempted to prompt a nonexistent memory.

"He abandoned you at the Waldorf. Five minutes before midnight. To deliver twins."

"I don't have a clue who or what you're..."

Understanding burst like a water balloon.

"Wait a sec. Are you talking about Sabrina's old boyfriend? Your buddy, who's now an ob-gyn doc?"

It was Logan's turn to look startled. He recovered faster than Devon had, though. His smile widened into a rueful grin.

"I take it you're not Sabrina Russo."

"No, Mr. Logan, I am *not*."

* * * * *

Be sure to look for
THE CEO'S CHRISTMAS PROPOSITION
by Merline Lovelace.
Available in November 2008
wherever books are sold,
including most bookstores, supermarkets,
drugstores and discount stores.

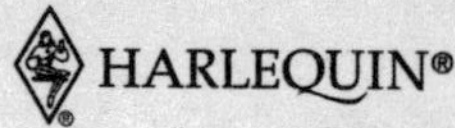

Blaze™

COMING NEXT MONTH

#429 KISS & TELL Alison Kent

In the world of celebrity tabloids, Caleb MacGregor is the best. Once he smells a scandal, he makes sure the world knows. And that's exactly what Miranda Kelly is afraid of. Hiding behind her stage name, Miranda hopes she'll avoid his notice. And she does—until she invites Caleb into her bed.

#430 UNLEASHED Lori Borrill

It's a wild ride in more ways than one when Jessica Beane is corralled into a road trip by homicide detective Rick Marshall. Crucial evidence is missing and Jess is the key to unlocking not just the case, but their pent-up passion, as well!

#431 A BODY TO DIE FOR Kimberly Raye
Love at First Bite, Bk. 3

Vampire Viviana Darland is in Skull Creek, Texas, looking for one thing—an orgasm. Or more specifically, the only man who's ever given her one, vampire Garret Sawyer. She knows her end is near, and wants one good climax before she goes. And she intends to get it—before Garret delivers on his promise to kill her....

#432 HER SEXIEST SURPRISE Dawn Atkins

He's the best birthday gift ever! When Chloe Baxter makes a sexy wish on her birthday candles, she never expects Riley Connelly—her secret crush—to appear. Nor does she expect him to give her the hottest night of her life. It's so hot, why share just one night?

#433 RECKLESS Tori Carrington
Indecent Proposals, Bk. 1

Heidi Joblowski isn't a woman to leave her life to chance. Her plan? To marry her perfect boyfriend, Jesse, and have several perfect children. Unfortunately, the only perfect thing in her life lately is the sex she's been having with Jesse's best friend Kyle....

#434 IN A BIND Stephanie Bond
Sex for Beginners, Bk. 2

Flight attendant Zoe Smythe is working her last shift, planning her wedding... and doing her best to ignore the sexual chemistry between her and a seriously sexy Australian passenger. But when she reads a letter she'd written in college, reminding her of her most private, erotic fantasies...all bets are off!

www.eHarlequin.com

HBCNM1008BPA